The Best Is
Yet to Be

MYSTERY
and the
MINISTER'S
WIFE®

The Best Is Yet to Be

EVE FISHER

GUIDEPOSTS
NEW YORK, NEW YORK

The Best Is Yet to Be

ISBN-13: 978-0-8249-4768-2

Published by Guideposts
16 East 34th Street
New York, New York 10016
www.guideposts.com

Distributed by Ideals Publications
2636 Elm Hill Pike, Suite 120
Nashville, Tennessee 37214

Library of Congress Cataloging-in-Publication Data.

Fisher, Eve.

  The best is yet to be / Eve Fisher.
      p. cm.—(Mystery and the minister's wife)
  ISBN 978-0-8249-4768-2
  1. Spouses of clergy—Fiction. 2. Clergy—Fiction. 3. Older people—Crimes against—Fiction. I. Title.
  PS3606.I7725B47 2009
  813'.6—dc22

                                        2008038012

Cover by Lookout Design Group
Interior design by Cris Kossow
Typeset by Nancy Tardi

Printed and bound in the United States of America

10 9 8 7 6 5 4 3 2 1

To all my friends in Madison, South Dakota,
and above all to Allan, with love and thanks.

Chapter One

K ate Hanlon entered the kitchen, shut the door behind her, and smiled a bit breathlessly at Joe Tucker, who was washing his hands at the sink. It was warm outside, but it was even warmer inside the old Bixby house this June morning.

She set a sack of rolls on the tile counter and smiled. "It must be lasagna today."

"It's about ready to come out of the oven," said Renee Lambert, looking up from the large pot of bubbling green beans she was stirring. "I hope those rolls are fresh, Kate."

Kate was too used to Renee to even sigh. "Fresh from the diner," she said brightly. She took off her light sweater and glanced around for Kisses, Renee's Chihuahua, who went everywhere with her.

Sure enough, there in a corner was Renee's huge tote, and the little dog's nose was sticking out of it. This was actually an improvement. When Renee had first started volunteering with Faith Briar's Faith Freezer Program, she had actually tried to dish up meals with her tote—and

Kisses—slung over one shoulder. Thankfully, Loretta Sweet, the owner of the Country Diner, had put an end to that, but only after threatening to call the health inspector. Loretta had also posted health requirements that included head coverings for cooks, and now Renee's synthetic blonde curls were covered by a white turban that had vivid butterflies sewn all over it. Joe Tucker had only a few white tufts of hair around his bald crown, but he wore a little white paper cap, which transformed him into a sort of backwoods Popeye, minus the pipe.

Kate went over to the supply cupboard and pulled out a box of hairnets. "No one else is cooking today?" she asked. She took a plain hairnet out of the box and put it on, carefully tucking in every strand of her strawberry-blonde hair.

"Eli Weston is supposed to be here," Joe said, shaking his head, "but he called to say he's running a bit late. A lady came over from Cookeville to look at end tables and hasn't left yet. And Dot Bagley is bringing dessert when she comes to make deliveries." He peered into the oven. "I think maybe another five minutes."

"It's ready now," Renee insisted, though she made no move to take it out of the oven. "And there's fruit salad in the refrigerator, Kate, so we'll need something to dish that up in."

"All right," Kate said, pulling the fruit salad out of the fridge, along with pats of butter for the rolls. She set them down on the table and went to the cupboard for small plastic cups with lids. There was only one stack left, so they'd need to pick up more.

As she walked toward the large bulletin board on the wall to write that down, Renee called out, "You might want to write out the delivery lists while you're over there!"

"Okay," Kate replied calmly.

The Faith Freezer Program was run from that bulletin board. The menus were posted there along with inventory lists, messages, and a calendar sign-up sheet for volunteers, both for cooking and delivery.

Faith Briar Church, where Kate's husband Paul was pastor, owned the little house, which had been donated by Mavis Bixby, and Kate had come up with the idea of using the kitchen to prepare and deliver meals to those in need. Now the Faith Freezer Program delivered about ten meals a day to shut-ins and invalids, as well as to sick parishioners and the elderly recovering from surgery. The Faith Freezer Program had become a necessary part of the Copper Mill community. Kate was constantly awed by how many people were willing to volunteer their time and energy.

She looked at the shopping list tacked to the bulletin board and saw that someone had already written down napkins and dish-washing liquid. That day's delivery volunteers were Dot Bagley, Amanda Bly, Junius Lawson, and his son, Matt. As Kate added plastic cups to the shopping list, she thought about how many of the volunteers were elderly themselves. Joe, Amanda, Junius, Dot, Martha Sinclair, Morty Robertson, and Renee were all in their sixties or seventies (even if Renee did insist she was only thirty-nine), and so were most of the others on the volunteer list.

This really wasn't surprising, since even though many Copper Mill residents volunteered freely of their time and resources, there was only so much time at their disposal. Most had jobs, like Kate's best friend Livvy Jenner, the town librarian, or they had businesses of their own, like Emma Blount, who owned the ice-cream shop. They all did what they could, but no one had the time to help out daily. Kate was lucky if she could help out twice a month, and the freezer program was originally her idea.

Although she was technically unemployed, she was a pastor's wife with a working stained-glass studio, not to mention the fact that since she and Paul had come to Copper Mill, she had been involved in solving the mysteries that seemed to crop up everywhere she went. There were days when she wondered how in the world she had ever managed to get everything done when she was working full-time in San Antonio. So much for the slower pace of small-town living. Life in Texas had been far less busy, it seemed, than it was in Tennessee.

"Sorry I'm late," Eli Weston called out as he came in. Behind him, a sudden gust of wind seemed to push a plump, gray-haired lady inside.

"I brought cupcakes," Dot Bagley gasped as Eli closed

the door firmly behind her and took the large box from her hands. "Chocolate."

Dot was one of the regulars at Betty's Beauty Parlor and a branch on the Copper Mill grapevine, but she was also a dedicated volunteer.

"Sounds heavenly," Kate said.

Dot nodded breathlessly and began fanning herself with her hands. "I'll be right over," she called out.

"Take your time," Eli called back.

Eli was one of the few younger volunteers for whom time wasn't a problem; running his antique store didn't seem to prevent him from volunteering for all sorts of causes. For a while Eli had been locked in a hard shell of anger and grief over the death of his fiancée and had been responsible for accidentally setting fire to Faith Briar Church. But he had been brought through that, by God's grace, to confession and reconciliation with the church and the community, and even more, with God. Faith Briar had been rebuilt, and Eli had become a full participant in church and community life. Kate knew it was a sense of immeasurable thankfulness that spurred him to devote as much of his time and energy to helping others as he could.

Kate went back over the delivery lists. There were twenty-five deliveries that day because of a flu outbreak that had hit Copper Mill's elderly population especially hard.

Joe was checking the oven again and Dot was chattering away about the latest news from the beauty shop, when suddenly Kate heard Kisses yapping, Joe yelping, metal crashing, Dot squealing, and a thud, followed by Renee screaming, "Look out!"

Kate whirled around and saw Joe sprawled on the floor, a pan of lasagna half emptied on him and the floor beside him, and Kisses licking at the mess.

"That blasted dog tripped me!" Joe glared at the pint-sized dog.

"Are you all right?" Eli asked.

"I think so."

"He's fine," Renee sniffed. "It's Kisses I'm worried about."

"How about the lasagna?" Kate asked.

Kisses yapped as Joe scrabbled around, trying to gain some footing on the slippery floor.

Renee snatched up her dog in her arms. "Don't you dare kick Kisses!"

"I wasn't kicking him, Renee," Joe snapped. "I'm just trying to get up!"

Renee kissed her dog's little head. "Just a bull in a china shop. Oh, poor little Kisses. Is Mama's Little Umpkins all right? Give Mama a kiss. You've scared him to death!"

The last comment, of course, was directed at Joe, who by now had a firm grip on his walking stick and was bringing himself upright.

"Are you sure you're all right, Joe?" Kate asked.

"Nothing a couple of aspirin and a pint of bleach won't cure," Joe said, ruefully looking down at his stained pants.

"Did it burn you?" Dot asked.

"Nah. I'm fine."

"What about the meals?" Renee asked. "What are we going to do? People are waiting on these."

"We've got two pans left," Eli said mildly. "We could just cut the pieces a little smaller and eke it out with the rolls."

"That will work fine," Kate said firmly. "Here, I'll cut the lasagna, and Joe, you go on home."

"Oh, nonsense," Joe said. "I'm fine. I can still pack meals."

"I'll start cleaning this up," Dot said and went over to the closet where the cleaning supplies were kept.

"Thank you, Dot," Kate said. "Thank heavens we've still got plenty of time to get these meals done." She started to cut up the lasagna, then looked at Renee, who was still holding her Chihuahua and cooing softly in his ear. "And can you put Kisses back in your bag, Renee, and start putting the fruit salad into cups?"

Renee sniffed but did as she was asked. Kate had finished cutting the lasagna when Emma Blount came in wearing a bright yellow shirt and tan pants. Yellow was Emma's favorite color, and she wore as much of it as possible, despite the fact that it clashed badly with her sallow skin and brown hair.

"Hi, Emma," Kate called. "I didn't see you on today's list."

"No," Emma replied, "but I thought I'd deliver Mama's dinner myself today."

"That's nice," Dot said.

Emma, a heavy woman in her late fifties, was never

neglectful of her eighty-two-old mother, Ada. She always made Ada's breakfast and supper, but lunch was usually out of the question. People wanted ice-cream sundaes, banana splits, malts, and shakes winter and summer, and the best place in town was Emma's Ice Cream shop.

"How are you doing, Emma?" Renee asked.

"Oh, I'm about worn out. Just rushed off my feet and I still haven't gotten my strength back from my operation."

"I'm sorry to hear that," Kate said as she put a square of lasagna in a container and passed it on to Renee and Joe to add the rest of the dinner. Kate didn't know exactly what kind of surgery Emma had had—she suspected female troubles, since Emma refused to talk about the details— but she did know that it had been in January, and now it was June. "Maybe you should go back to your doctor."

"I have." Emma dabbed at her eyes with a tissue. "And all he says is that everything's fine and I should just lose some weight." Her double chin quivered indignantly.

"They say that to everyone." Dot sighed.

"I have just the opposite problem," Renee said. "My doctor's always on me to gain weight, but what can I do? I eat like a bird. Always have."

"Here you go, Emma," Eli said, handing her the boxed dinner.

"Nobody knows the suffering I go through," Emma continued. "Thank you, Eli. I swear I'd go to a specialist, but that would mean going to Knoxville and then who'd look after Mama? Oh my, look at the time. I've got to run. See y'all later!"

Renee watched Emma leave, then said, "That poor woman is just a martyr to her mother."

Kate almost choked as she thought about Renee's ninety-two-year-old mother, the redoubtable Caroline Beauregard Johnston. She'd moved in with Renee while she was healing from a broken hip and was still there, just as much a queen bee as ever. Since there wasn't much of the martyr in Renee, the two had had some memorable exchanges over Kisses (Caroline hated dogs), food (Caroline wouldn't touch "any of that freezer slop"), friends (Caroline didn't approve of Renee's), churches (Caroline went to St. Lucy's Episcopal Church), and almost everything else. The only things they agreed on were bridge and that the world was, in general, going to the dogs and had been ever since the Civil War. Or, as Caroline called it, the War of Northern Aggression.

"Well, let's get crackin', folks," Joe said. "Only twenty-four to go."

ELI WAS SNAPPING the last lid onto a plastic container when Amanda Bly, Junius Lawson, and his son, Matt, arrived.

"After you, madam," Junius said, holding the door for Amanda.

"Hello, all. My, but it smells good in here," Amanda said, her blue eyes twinkling in her crepe-paper face. She was a tiny woman, always beautifully groomed, her white hair done in a neat French knot, her white gloves immaculate. "What is it?"

"Lasagna," Kate said.

"As you can tell by my pants," Joe added.

Amanda raised her eyebrows and turned to Eli. "Tell me, did I see a red velvet settee in your shop window?"

"Yes, ma'am. Interested?"

"Just nostalgic. My mother used to have one just like it." Amanda turned her attention toward Renee. "And how are you doing?"

"Well, I'll be doing a lot better after I get my hair done," Renee said, whisking off her turban and running her extremely long manicured nails—painted a bright peony on this occasion—through her metallic-blonde curls. "I wouldn't have set foot outside the house looking the way I do if it wasn't my day to volunteer."

"Now you know you always look like a breath of spring," Junius said gallantly.

Renee actually giggled. "Why, Mr. Lawson, I do declare," she flirted. "You could turn a girl's head saying things like that."

"Just telling the truth," Junius said and, leaning over, whispered something to Renee that made her giggle again.

"Could I have my delivery list?" Matt Lawson asked Kate brusquely.

She looked over at Junius, who was chatting easily with Renee and Amanda, and thought about how different father and son were. Junius was a tall, thin, distinguished man with a handsome, hawkish face set under a thick shock of white hair; his son was awkward and stuffy, with an average build and average looks. While Junius sparkled with personality, Matt never seemed to want to talk.

"Of course," Kate said.

Matt simply waited without saying anything. Kate had noticed before that Matt simply didn't seem to know how to make small talk or exchange the friendly greetings and inquiries that oiled the wheels of small-town life. She handed Matt his list and watched him quickly go over it. He was supposed to be excellent with figures, which was good, since he was an investment adviser at the bank. But his lack of people skills must have been a handicap. Of course, as long as people were making money, they'd overlook it.

Matt nodded, went over to the table, and started piling meals into a flat box.

Kate followed him. "Here are your lists, Dot, Amanda, Junius."

"Thank you, Kate," Junius said. He looked at his list and said, "Joshua Parsons! I know he'll try to get me to play checkers."

"Well, if you'd like, I'll take it to him," Joe said. "I'm always up for a good game of checkers."

"No, no," Junius said. " I need the experience."

Amanda, who had been looking at her list, smiled and said, "Oh good, I get to see Nell. She is such a delight. She always asks me to play the piano for her, and I do believe she enjoys it almost as much as I do."

"Of course she does," Kate said. "You're a wonderful pianist."

"I'd love to play ragtime," Dot said, hooking her purse strap over her shoulder. "The way your fingers just fly across those keys!"

"Yes, well, they don't fly as much as they used to, but I keep on going." Amanda smiled bravely, showing her hands, her fingers twisted by arthritis.

By now Eli had packed up her dinners in a box.

"Would you like some help?" Joe asked.

Amanda bent down as if she hadn't heard him and started to lift the box, but it was obviously too much for her.

Junius snapped his fingers and Matt came over. "Help out a bit, Son."

"Oh sure." Matt picked up the box, and Amanda, Dot, and Junius followed him outside, calling out their farewells.

"Well!" Renee declared, picking up her tote and slinging it over her shoulder so that Kisses' head was almost under her chin. "Did you ever see such an obvious maneuver in all your life?"

Joe Tucker was looking out the window bleakly. Kate had noticed at other times that Joe and Amanda didn't seem to get along, and now Amanda had ignored Joe the whole time she had been in the kitchen. For the life of her, Kate couldn't understand why. True, Joe was an old backwoodsman with all the polish of his hand-hewn log cabin and Amanda was like a tiny bit of finished porcelain. But they had so much in common: They had both been born in Copper Mill, they both loved music and they both attended Faith Briar Church. There had to be a reason, but Kate hadn't lived in Copper Mill long enough to know all the townspeople and their histories.

"Some women aren't happy unless *all* the men are flocking around them *all* the time," Renee was saying to Kisses. "Isn't that right, Little Umpkins?"

"Well, I promised to meet Morty Robertson down at the diner," Joe said. "Want to join us, Eli?"

"I can't. I need to get back to the shop. I've got a couple of ladies coming over from Lenoir City at twelve thirty."

"Somebody's got to clean up here," Renee reminded them. "And I have an appointment at the beauty shop, so I can't stay."

"Everybody just run along," Kate said. "I'll clean up. You've all done a great job."

"Thank you," Renee said, walking toward the door. "Ta ta!"

"Good-bye, Renee!" Kate called, feeling a twinge of relief.

"Now, are you sure you can handle all this?" Joe asked.

"Yes," Kate said, smiling. "You need to go change your pants."

Kate washed the pots and pans, the fruit bowl, and the utensils and scrubbed the table and countertops. The sun poured in through the window over her sudsy hands, and she promised herself a walk downtown when she was all done. Maybe she'd stop by the library and see Livvy Jenner. That would cheer her up. She realized that she needed some cheering. The wonderful feelings she had had when the Faith Freezer Program started seemed very far away.

But feelings aren't facts, Kate reminded herself. The facts were that the Faith Freezer Program had delivered hundreds of meals and the house had been a temporary home for at least a dozen people, giving them a start toward new lives. Both were important parts of Faith Briar's ministry and Kate's personal ministry.

But the morning hadn't gone as well as she'd hoped. And though Renee had been a bit irritating, she was one of the program's most dedicated volunteers and truly was far more important to its daily operation than Kate was. Kate took a deep breath and remembered the verse, *"The Lord himself goes before you and will be with you; he will never leave you nor forsake you. Do not be afraid; do not be discouraged."*

She smiled and turned to see that Emma Blount was back.

"Emma! Was your mother's meal okay?"

"Oh, it was fine. But I'm so glad you're still here," Emma said, laying her purse on the table and slowly lowering herself into a chair. "I was afraid you might have gone."

"Not yet," Kate said brightly, although she felt apprehensive. Emma looked worried. Something was wrong. "Would you like some coffee? I could put the pot on."

"That's okay. I need to get back to the shop soon."

"I'm afraid we don't have any leftovers to offer you, but there are a couple of rolls."

"Oh, I'm fine. I never eat lunch. I just nibble all day at the shop. They say that having lots of little meals is better for you than three big meals a day, and I believe it. I don't ever get indigestion because I really don't eat that much, just a broken cookie or a couple of nuts or a spoonful of the new flavor."

"What is the new flavor?" Kate asked.

"Pistachio cream. It's wonderful."

"I'll have to try some." She sat down across from Emma and said, "Now, what can I do for you?"

"Kate, I don't know how to say this, but . . . I'm afraid someone's been stealing from Mama."

"Stealing?" Kate was shocked. "What? How?"

"Well, I've noticed a few things missing. Mama had a lovely brooch, just rhinestones, but it was really pretty, one of those big old-fashioned ones, like a starburst. And there was a book of poetry I used to read when I was a little girl. I can't find them anywhere. And I'm sure a few other things have gone missing too."

Kate sighed. Everyone knew that Ada Blount was in the early stages of Alzheimer's, even if Emma could never bring herself to say the word.

"Emma," she said gently, "don't you think it's possible that your mother simply misplaced them? Put the brooch in the bathroom cabinet, and the book in, well, her bedroom closet? Or a dresser? Or even in the trash? By accident? Not meaning to, of course."

Emma looked down at her lap. "Maybe."

"So maybe if you really searched . . ."

"It's more than that, though," Emma said. "There's money gone. All her bills are paid through automatic withdrawal, because, well, you know."

Kate nodded.

"But she still has a checking account, for groceries and odds and ends. Well, I usually balance the checkbook every month, but the last couple of months I wasn't able to because of my surgery. And you know, I'm still not feeling one hundred percent. How I get through the day, I don't know. I'm simply exhausted by the end of it."

"I'm sure you are," Kate said soothingly. "But what about Ada?"

"Well, I finally sat down night before last to balance her accounts and I found that she'd written six checks to cash. And all of them were for either two or three thousand dollars!"

Kate gasped.

"Frankly, and I'd only say this to you, because you and the pastor, well . . . that's all the money Mama had. It wiped out all her savings."

"Oh no!" Kate said. "Did she have any explanation?"

"First she said she couldn't remember. Then this morning she said she'd invested it!" Emma's chin was trembling. "And she won't—or can't—say anything else. All her savings gone!"

"But who on earth took the checks? Who cashed them? Have they been cashed? She didn't just write them and tear them up, did she?"

"Oh no. They were cashed. I called the bank. She's down to almost nothing."

Kate put her hands to her face. "Oh, Emma, I'm so sorry. But who on earth could have done this?"

"That's what I want to know! I've checked her telephone bills and she hasn't been making any long-distance phone calls. You know, to those scam artists you hear about all the time. And she hasn't been sending anything by mail, except birthday cards, and I get those for her and get them ready for her to sign, and then I mail them. She doesn't get any visitors other than the ladies from church, and I've known them all my life. The only other people who come into the house are the people who deliver her meals. So I think it's got to be one of them. One of the volunteers from the Faith Freezer Program."

Chapter Two

K ate sat back, winded. "One of our volunteers?" she finally gasped. "A thief?"

"Who else could it be? It's certainly not the postman," Emma said indignantly.

"No, it wouldn't be Fish," Kate agreed.

"And I know it couldn't be any of the ladies from the church. So it has to be one of the volunteers who delivers meals. I don't know what to do except go to the police, and I don't want to do that . . ."

"*Mmm,*" Kate murmured noncommittally. "What name was on the back of the canceled checks?"

"That's just it. I don't know," Emma said. "Now that everything's electronic, Mama just gets copies of her checks, and they only show the front side, not the endorsement. I've ordered copies of the checks from the bank, but who knows how long that will take. They have to come from Chattanooga. And that's if they haven't been destroyed already."

Kate nodded. "Have you told anyone else about this?"

"No, not exactly . . ."

Kate held her breath. Emma was one of the regulars at Betty's Beauty Parlor, the hub of gossip in Copper Mill.

"I asked the ladies at church if Mama had been acting a little funny lately, but they thought I meant, well, you know . . . And I did mention the brooch to Betty when I was having my hair done the other day, but that's all. And the book. And do you know there are other people who've noticed things going missing? We talked about that a good while," Emma said thoughtfully. "Renee Lambert said there was a lot of that going on a few years ago and they traced it back to a couple of school kids."

Kate nodded. "But you didn't tell them about the money."

"No. I didn't even know about it then and I'd never mention something like that down there. To be honest, my first thought was to keep it quiet. I don't want anyone laughing at Mama."

"No one would laugh, Emma," Kate said, horrified.

"Oh yes, they would," she said glumly. "They'd be all pity and shock, but they'd be snickering about Mama being taken in by some con man. You should have heard them back when Mabel Trout got taken by those guys who pour fake asphalt. Oh, Sheriff Roberts investigated and all that, but you could tell he thought she was just plain stupid to have fallen for it."

"I'm sure he didn't," Kate said.

Emma rolled her eyes. "Oh yes, he did. I've never felt the same about him ever since. So I thought that since

you've looked into a few mysteries around town, maybe . . .
Well, you've always found out some things nobody else
could. And if you'd look into it, we could keep things quiet
for a little while."

"I'll be happy to look into it."

"Thanks, Kate. And you'll let me know what you find
out?"

Kate nodded. "And you'll let me know as soon as you
get those canceled checks?"

"I will. Oh my, look at the time. I've got to get back to
the shop," Emma said, gathering her things. "You know, I
feel a little better already. Though when I . . . I mean when
we find out who did this . . ."

"I know. And we will find out. Don't worry." Kate managed a smile as she watched Emma get into her car and
drive off. Her mind was whirling, and she was torn
between going home or going to the church; it was the
same distance either way, since the Bixby house, the parsonage, and the church formed an *L*, with the Bixby
house in the middle. Now the white walls and steeple of
Faith Briar seemed to invite her to spend a few minutes in
quiet prayer before tackling the problem.

Just as she was stepping out the kitchen door, a black
Lincoln pulled up and Junius Lawson stuck his head out
the window.

"Just heading back from Old Man Parsons' and I saw
Emma pulling out. Everything okay with Ada?"

"She's fine," Kate called back.

"Good. Well, I'm all done and off to the diner for a
piece of pie. You had any lunch yet?"

"No, I haven't," Kate said. "I haven't had time."

"Well, it's too late to cook anything. Come on with me. I'll give you a lift."

"That sounds great," Kate said, thinking this was a good way to kill two birds with one stone. She could start by talking to Junius, and maybe Joe Tucker was still there as well. He rarely made deliveries, but he might have heard something about things mysteriously disappearing. "Give me a second to get my things."

"Need any help?"

"No, thanks!" she called out.

Dashing back inside, Kate got her light sweater and her handbag, then stepped outside and locked the door. Junius was standing by the car and opened the door for her.

"Thank you," she said.

"My pleasure."

"This must be brand new," Kate commented. "It still has that wonderful new-car smell."

Junius beamed, and as he pulled out onto Mountain Laurel Road, he told her in such depth all about why, where, and how he'd gotten it that Kate amusedly pegged Junius as one of those grown-up boys who loves his toys. Especially if the toys were big, sleek, and powerful. Her conclusion was confirmed when they parked outside the Country Diner next to a huge black Chevy Silverado pickup, obviously brand new.

"Well, will you look at that!" Junius said, getting out of his car, his eyes glued to the truck. "I wonder whose that is?"

"I don't know," Kate commented, heading toward the diner entrance.

Junius pulled himself together and ran ahead to open the door for her.

"It sure is quite a vehicle," he said, glancing back.

Kate smiled and walked inside. It was after one o'clock and only a few people were left at the diner, leisurely finishing their pie and coffee. She saw Joe Tucker and Morty Robertson, sitting in a back booth. They had definitely lingered over their meal.

"Kate, Junius!" Joe called out. "Come and join us."

"We'd love to," Kate said. She slid in next to Joe, and Junius sat next to Morty.

"You should never bid four no trumps," Junius said solemnly, and Morty roared.

Kate looked at Joe, who shrugged and said, "Some old joke between them. Don't even try to figure it out."

Junius looked around the diner, then he sighed and said, "Well, I don't see anyone else in here, though I can't believe that either of you two dug into your wallets deep enough to buy a beauty like that truck sitting outside."

Joe laughed. "'Tain't neither one of us," he said as LuAnne Matthews bustled over with fresh silverware rolled in napkins.

"Hello, Kate, Junius," she said.

"Junius is admiring your new vehicle," Joe teased.

LuAnne blushed and smiled. She patted her rich red hair—obviously freshly done—and said, "It's somethin' else, isn't it? Eat your hearts out, boys." Then she asked Kate, "You want coffee or iced tea, Kate?"

"Iced tea, please, LuAnne."

"Sweet?"

Kate nodded.

"Today's special is ham and biscuits and gravy."

"I think I'll go a little lighter than that," Kate said. "A chicken-salad sandwich on white toast, please."

"Fries?" LuAnne asked.

"I don't think so," Kate said, shaking her head. "Just chips."

"Don't tell me you're watchin' your weight," LuAnne protested. Heavyset herself, the only thing that daunted LuAnne's cheerfulness was dieters. Her attitude was that food was for eating and if it put weight on you, well, that was just something you had to accept.

"No, just my cholesterol," Kate reassured her.

"How about you, Junius?" LuAnne asked.

Junius spread his hands and said dramatically, "LuAnne, honey, I would love a piece of apple pie à la mode and a cup of coffee deeply, deeply leaded. With extra cream." He smiled at Kate. "My reward for a hard morning's work."

LuAnne grinned and went over to the pass-through window that opened into the kitchen, placed the tickets there, and whirled the carousel around. Loretta Sweet's hand came out and the tickets vanished.

"So, what are you two gentlemen chatting about?" Junius asked.

"Life, the universe, and everything," Joe said expansively.

LuAnne set a tall glass of iced tea in front of Kate and passed Junius his coffee.

"Specifically, the summer concert series in the park," Morty added. "Joe's trying to talk the Elks into doing root-beer floats—"

"As a fund-raiser," Joe interrupted. "You know, a dollar a float, all the money to go to charity."

"They'd have to be awfully small floats to make a profit," Kate pointed out.

"I said that too." Morty nodded.

"Okay, so they're small. It's for charity."

"Why not just charge two dollars or even two fifty?" Junius asked.

"I asked that too," Morty said.

"Because," Joe explained, "there are an awful lot of cheapskates in this town who wouldn't pay two dollars for Häagen-Dazs, much less the kind of ice cream we'd be serving. And we want to get into their wallets. And pocket-books. And savings accounts."

Kate twitched.

"Did I bump you?" Joe asked.

"No," Kate replied.

LuAnne slid Kate's lunch plate in front of her and Junius' pie in front of him. "Here you go. You let me know if you want anything else."

"The keys to your truck?" Junius asked.

"In your dreams." LuAnne laughed.

"Thanks, LuAnne." Kate's stomach growled, and she said a quick silent prayer. Picking up one sandwich half, she took a bite. It was delicious. She hadn't realized how hungry she was.

"So, how did the deliveries go?" she asked Junius in between bites.

"Just fine," he said, spearing the point of his pie. "I beat Old Man Parsons at checkers."

"You never did!" Joe exclaimed.

"Ask him," Junius said proudly. "And I made my other deliveries. You ask me, I think some of these folks are malingering. They're over the flu; they just want the food and the company. When the sun comes out like today, they want to be out and about, and since they can't, company's the next best thing. Happy to give it to them, though. *Mmm*. This pie is heaven. LuAnne!" he called out, "you tell Loretta that's the best pie yet."

LuAnne laughed. "I will."

"I heard that." Loretta stuck her head out the window. "Try the rhubarb."

"Another day," Junius called back. "I'll tell you what, a day like this, a pie like this, just makes you glad to be alive, doesn't it?"

"Amen," Joe said.

"I'm always glad I'm alive," Morty said. "Every morning I wake up, take a deep breath, pinch myself, and say, 'Thank you, Lord, for another day.' Then I get up and waste as much of it as I can."

Everybody laughed.

"No, no, no," Junius said. "You've got to have a system when you're retired. Parcel out your day and live by a schedule."

"I had enough schedule when I was working," Morty

replied. "Now I get up early, do my chores, have lunch with any layabout I can find, and then go home to watch *Oprah*."

Kate almost choked on her sandwich.

"What's so funny?"

"I just never thought of you being an *Oprah* fan," she admitted.

"I have hidden depths," Morty assured her.

"I'm sure you do. Otherwise, you wouldn't volunteer as much as you do," Kate replied. She knew Morty volunteered at the library, with the Faith Freezer Program and at a number of other places. "The same goes for all of you. I know everyone at Faith Freezer appreciates all your help."

"It's our pleasure," Junius said. "And I know I'm speaking for all of us when I say that we get much more out of it than we put in."

Morty and Joe nodded, and Morty added, "It's a great program. I don't know how some of the people we serve ever managed before."

"Oh, we're changing lives," Joe said. "I don't think Mindy Corson lived on anything but peanut-butter sandwiches and Gatorade before this got started. Not that there's anything wrong with that, and I'm sure it would have kept her alive for years. But . . ."—his tone became very serious—"I'm proud to be part of the program."

"So am I," Kate said. She wiped her lips with her napkin, took a deep breath, and said, "Tell me, have any of you heard of anything, well, going missing?"

When the three men looked puzzled, she went on. "I

heard that some people have complained that things have disappeared. Vanished. Mysteriously." Her heart thudded as she waited for a response.

All three men continued looking puzzled.

Joe was the first to speak. "Disappeared?"

Kate nodded.

"What, they thinking someone's been stealing things?"

"It's been mentioned," Kate admitted.

"*Pshaw*," Joe said. "I can't believe that."

"Neither can I," Morty said, shaking his head. "I haven't heard anything like that at all."

"Neither have I," Junius said, picking up his fork and spearing the last piece of pie. "I'm sure it's nothing. It's all too easy to lose things once you get to a certain age. And that describes most of the people I deliver to." He chewed his pie and swallowed. "Shoot, it happens to me. I lost my watch two days ago and I haven't found it yet. Who knows? It could be anywhere. And if I set it down in the kitchen, I'll never find it because I don't cook," he explained. "I'm sure whatever's gone missing will turn up again, or if it doesn't, it's at the bottom of a huge pile of stuff that would take an act of Congress to shift."

"That's true," Joe said. "Now, take Mindy Corson. You ever been in her place?"

Kate shook her head. Small as Copper Mill was, there were still a lot of people she hadn't met.

"She's the world's worst pack rat. I believe that's why she gave up cooking. It's not that she can't cook; she just can't find the stove."

Kate laughed, and Joe smiled at her.

"Do you need to get going?" Kate asked Junius.

"Unfortunately, yes," he said.

"I really should go too," she said.

"So should I," Joe chimed in.

"Everybody's deserting me," Morty complained as the three rose from the table.

"I've got a schedule to keep," Junius reminded him. "It's time for me to go rest up. You don't look as good as I do at my age without getting plenty of beauty sleep." Then he leaned in toward Morty and said, "Try it sometime. Might even improve your looks."

Junius winked and walked away, leaving Morty roaring with laughter.

"He's got you there," Joe said, leaving a tip on the table.

"See you later," Morty called.

Kate said good-bye and followed Joe over to the counter where LuAnne was gazing out the window, watching Junius walk jauntily out the door and down the street.

Joe pulled out his wallet and took out a couple of bills. He glanced at Kate as he dug around in his pocket for a handful of change. "Now don't you be worrying yourself sick about this," he said comfortingly. "Whatever's happened, it'll come right. I've seen a lot and I know."

"Thanks, Joe." Kate smiled.

"Nothing to thank me for . . . Just the truth." Joe put some change on top of his ticket and the rest back in his pocket. Then he tapped the ticket and money and said, "It's all there, LuAnne."

THE BEST IS YET TO BE   29

"Thanks, Joe," LuAnne said, not taking her eyes off Junius.

"See you later, Kate," Joe said, and left.

"You'd never dream he was in his seventies lookin' at him walk, now would you?" LuAnne asked. "And he can dance too."

"Really?" Kate asked. "Joe?"

"No, Junius," LuAnne said, taking Kate's ticket. "From what I hear. The morning after every senior-citizens' dance, the women come in here for coffee, and all you hear is them goin' on about Junius Lawson. Poor things. Most men their age can't get up on a dance floor any more than once or twice. But Junius can dance all night long and he dances with everybody. Makes him really popular."

"I'll bet it does," Kate chuckled, taking her change. "By the way, congratulations on your new truck. It's beautiful."

"Thanks," LuAnne said, blushing again, to Kate's surprise. "I still can't believe it's mine."

"Well, I'll see you later," Kate said.

"See you!" LuAnne called after her.

Outside, Kate took a deep breath of fresh June air and felt much better. The food had helped, but the conversation had helped even more. There were so many innocent explanations for what might have happened to the missing items and Ada's money. Kate remembered a great-aunt of legend, who her mother had always said kept her money in the family Bible.

"So, just remember," her mother had concluded every time, "never, ever throw out an old book, no matter how worm-eaten it is, at least not without looking through it carefully. You never know what might be in it."

Kate laughed. Maybe Ada had cashed those checks herself and stashed the money in her house somewhere. Wouldn't it be wonderful if that was the solution to this mystery?

Kate thought she'd head down to the library to see Livvy for a minute. Perhaps they could make arrangements for a walk the next day. As she walked down Smith Street, she saw Eli through the window of his antiques shop, talking to a couple of elderly ladies. The clock at the corner of the Town Green said two fifteen. She was just about to cross Main Street when she saw Renee Lambert, who had obviously just come from fresh ministrations at Betty's Beauty Parlor.

"Kate!" Renee called out. "I want to talk to you!"

Kate's heart sank. But she crossed the street and went over to Renee, who was standing in front of the Mercantile, Copper Mill's general store. "Your hair looks lovely," she said.

"Yes, I think Betty did an especially nice job today." Renee fluffed her hair.

"Very nice," Kate agreed. "I'm just on my way to the library."

"Well, before you go, what I want to know is what's all this about thefts?"

"Thefts?" Kate faltered.

"Yes, thefts!" Renee said loudly.

Kate looked around quickly, but nobody was nearby.

Renee continued, "The other day Emma told us that Ada lost a rhinestone brooch. And today Dot Bagley said that Mabel Trout told her that her silver tea service is missing. Sugar bowl and creamer both vanished into thin air. Somebody's stolen them."

"Did somebody break into her place? Is anything else missing?" Kate asked. "Has she reported it to the police?"

"Nobody's broken into anything," Renee said. "If they had, everybody in town would know about it. Now, we all agreed that it has to be somebody who's—"

"By we, you mean the beauty-shop ladies?" Kate interrupted, exasperated at the thought of the gossipy group.

"Of course. Somebody who's in and out of her place, looking like they're above suspicion. And I was thinking, it's about time we started doing those background thingamajiggers on our volunteers. Everybody would feel a lot safer."

"Renee," Kate said, horrified, "you didn't say that at the beauty shop, did you?"

"I most certainly did not," Renee sniffed. "I wouldn't dream of dragging Faith Briar's name through the mud. But you mark my words, something needs to be done. The Faith Freezer Program was your idea, and I'm not saying it wasn't a good one, but now we've got everybody and their brother just marching through everybody's house without a by your leave. It's our responsibility to do something about it. I'll be happy to help you look into it."

"Well . . ." Kate began, her heart sinking.

"No problem at all," Renee assured her. "You know I'm always happy to help out. I know everybody in town and I can ask around. You do the same and let's just see what we can turn up between us."

Renee marched off, trailing a cloud of Estée Lauder's Youth-Dew behind her, Kisses' tail wagging under her shoulder blade.

Kate took a deep breath and let it out slowly. Renee was right about one thing: She needed to do something. Instead of going to see Livvy, she walked past the Mercantile and into Emma's Ice Cream Shop.

"Kate!" Emma exclaimed. In her yellow blouse and apron, she almost blended into the bright yellow walls of her shop. She lowered her voice, even though there was no one else in the shop. "Have you heard anything?"

"No, but I was wondering if maybe you could take a few minutes off so we can go see your mother. I'd like to talk to her myself, and it would be good if . . ." Kate's voice trailed off.

"If I reintroduced you?" Emma asked.

Kate nodded.

"You're probably right," Emma said, taking off her apron. "Mama just doesn't remember people as well as she used to. I'll put the sign on the door."

A few minutes later, they were walking down Ashland Street, past Livvy's house, to the corner at Quarry Road. Ada Blount's small house was painted bright yellow— undoubtedly Emma's choice—with white gingerbread trim and white spindle-work posts. An iron lawn chair, painted white, sat on the minuscule porch. The narrow walkway from porch to street was flanked by manicured green grass, and the whole property was bordered with bridal wreath, which had obviously never been trimmed, its white blossoms foaming up and out like fountains.

"How beautiful!" Kate said as they walked by the bridal wreath.

"Thank you," Emma said proudly.

"You must put in a lot of work here."

"Oh, I try to make things nice for Mama." Emma opened the door. "Of course, I can't do as much as I used to before my operation. But I try . . . Mama! You awake?"

Kate could hear the television even on the porch, and as they walked into the living room, the sound became deafening. The air was a little stuffy, as if the windows hadn't been opened since the previous year, but the room was light and airy, with flocked beige wallpaper and white trim. Ada was sitting in a plush, gold, overstuffed arm-chair between two tables piled high with magazines, papers, and miscellaneous objects.

"Mama," Emma said cheerfully, "I brought someone to see you."

Ada smiled happily at them and started to rise with difficulty because of her hugely swollen legs. *Heart problems*, Kate thought.

"No, don't get up," she urged. Kate looked around for a place to sit, but most of the furniture was stacked to over-flowing. She wondered if Mindy Corson's place was worse than this.

"Here, let me clear off the settee," Emma said, moving a pile of magazines.

"Now be careful! I haven't finished with those!" Ada called out.

"Mama," Emma said, "I'll put them right here where you can get to them." She whispered to Kate, "She never does read them all, but she likes to have them around."

Kate nodded. She was beginning to feel more hopeful that perhaps theft wasn't the problem, at least as far as the small things. Emma might keep the outside perfect, but the inside was obviously more than she could keep up with.

"Now, Mama, do you need anything?" Emma asked.

"No, I'm fine. Now who are you?" Ada asked, turning to Kate.

"This is Kate Hanlon, our pastor's wife. Remember? Pastor Hanlon, at Faith Briar?"

"But what happened to Pastor Jacobs?" Ada asked.

"He retired, Mama. A while back. Remember? Before the fire?"

"Fire? What fire?"

"The one at the church."

"Oh." Ada shook her head. "I don't remember any fire. I remember when Cousin Eddie set fire to Uncle Martin's barn and burned it to the ground." She turned to Kate and shook her head again. "Smoking. I warned Uncle Martin, but she doted on that boy. Now you look like Aunt Icey. She had strawberry-blonde hair that she wore all piled up on her head like a movie star. You must be Marybeth. You remember Marybeth, Emma. She married the blacksmith . . . No, that was Lucy. Or was it—"

"Mama, this is Kate Hanlon. She's married to our new pastor, Paul Hanlon."

"New pastor? Oh yes! He's a lovely man. He comes to

see me every week. And you've come once or twice too, haven't you?"

"Yes, I have," Kate said.

"Now I remember." Ada turned to Emma. "Why didn't you say who she was?"

Emma grimaced slightly.

Ada turned back to Kate. "Would you like some iced tea? I know Emma's got a pitcher in the fridge . . ."

Ada started to get up again, but Kate stopped her. "No, please, I'm fine. How about you?"

"Oh, I've got some right here." Ada looked up at Emma. "Are you going to sit down or just flutter around like a bird?"

"No, Mama. I've got to get back to the shop. But you and Kate have a nice visit."

"We certainly will," Ada said. "You get on out of here."

Emma kissed her mother on the cheek and waved good-bye to Kate. Ada watched her go, then she sank back in her chair and smiled. "She's the sweetest little thing a mother could hope for."

"I'm sure she is," Kate replied. "You know, she's a bit worried about you."

"She is? Why?"

"Well, she told me about some things that are missing."

"Oh, those." Ada waved her hand as if it was insignificant. "Emma fusses too much. She was worrying me half to death about a brooch that I never really liked to begin with. Horace gave it to me when we were first engaged, and I was so disappointed. I never liked rhinestones. Too gaudy. Not that I told him. It would have hurt his feelings. And now it's gone and I say good riddance. The only reason I worried about it was because I knew Emma liked it. But after all, it's not like it's worth much of anything." Ada leaned toward Kate and whispered, "She makes such a fuss."

"I think she's more worried about the checks," Kate said carefully.

"Checks? What checks?"

"She said you wrote some checks to cash? Large checks?"

"Oh yes!" Ada remembered. "I did. I had a little nest egg. Not a lot, but something, just in case anything ever happened. Not that anything ever does. And not that I depended on it, because I do have Horace's pension and I get Social Security, and Emma is just the sweetest girl. She takes such good care of me."

"And the nest egg?" Kate asked.

"Huh? Oh yes. Well, it was just laying there, doing nothing, and when I saw a chance to invest it, why, that's what I did."

"Invest it? In what?"

"Investments. You know."

"Who invested it for you?" Kate asked gently.

"Oh, now what is that fellow's name? He keeps coming around. Bringing things. Talks about investments all the time. That's his business, you know."

Matt Lawson's impassive face flashed across Kate's mind. *Oh no*, she thought. *Please, not him.*

"And he told me how I could double my money. So I did."

"Can you remember his name?" Kate asked and held her breath as Ada sat there and thought.

"I'm sorry, honey. I'm just no good with names any-more. Unless it's someone I knew as a child. It's funny how you get. I can remember every one of my cousins from when I was a little girl and I couldn't stand half of them."

Kate was tempted to list the men of the Faith Freezer Program for Ada but stopped herself. The last thing she wanted to do was plant a name in Ada's failing memory. "But when this man comes, doesn't he introduce himself?"

"Well, I'm sure he did, but I don't always pay atten-tion." Ada leaned over and confessed, "I know I'm going to forget, so I just don't bother remembering." She sat back and sighed. "Oh, but he was so nice. He said he'd double my money for me." She smiled at Kate. "Isn't it wonderful? I can hardly wait!"

Chapter Three

K ate walked home slowly from Ada's, both because she felt too tired to walk at her usual quick pace and because she needed time to think about what to do next. It was quite a long walk, so she had plenty of time to think. *Investments* . . . The only person in Copper Mill who handled investments was Matt Lawson. Of course, there were investment advisers over in Pine Ridge, Kate was sure, but they didn't volunteer with the Faith Freezer Program.

Matt Lawson. The only thing she could think of was to go talk to him. But what was she going to say? "Did you steal money from Ada Blount? Did you con a sick old woman into writing checks that can't be traced?" It was ridiculous, and she couldn't see it eliciting a confession of guilt. But she was going to have to start somewhere . . .

Kate walked past the sheriff's office and thought grimly that if Sheriff Roberts could read her mind, he'd be out of his office like a shot to follow her. Luckily his car wasn't there. She took a deep breath and crossed

Hamilton Road. She could see the Bixby house on Smoky Mountain Road, with Faith Briar Church across from it.

Lord, you're going to have to help me. I don't know what I'm going to do. I'm going to talk to him, but I don't want to. Kate remembered a prayer from one of her morning devotionals and whispered it: "Lord, help me when I don't know what to do, and help me even more when I know what to do but don't want to do it." That about summed up her situation.

She walked past the Bixby house and up to the parsonage. It was a small, three bedroom ranch, and when she and Paul had first set foot in the decorating disaster it had been, all she could think was that God had a considerable sense of humor. Since then Kate had stripped the ceilings of their popcorn texture, reworked every wall and window of the oversized living room, replaced the fluorescent lights, and completely transformed the third bedroom into her stained-glass studio. It had become home, warm and welcoming, and never did she need it as much as right then.

She took off her light sweater and set it and her purse down on the table in the entryway. Then she walked over to the sliding-glass doors in the living room and looked out at the maple in their backyard, then up to the trees that covered the hills behind their home. The redbud and dogwood were no longer blooming, but the giant tulip poplars were full of living green and orange sconces. Kate especially looked forward to when the mimosa flowered, the trees draped in pink feathers, although she'd been told in

no uncertain terms by Old Man Parsons that mimosas were
nothing but pests and she should dig them out. That was
never going to happen. If anything, she decided she would
plant some in their yard, where she could enjoy them.

"Hey, good lookin'."

Kate jumped. Paul stood in the doorway wearing a
bathrobe, a towel draped around his neck, his hair wet
and spiky from a shower.

"Oh! You startled me!" she gasped.

"I'm sorry. Are you okay?" he asked, walking over to her.

"I'm fine," she said, kissing him. "Just . . . How was
your day?"

"Busy. I worked out some notes for my sermon, visited
a few people, that sort of thing. What have you been up
to? Get any work done in your studio?"

"No." Kate shook her head. "This morning was my day
to volunteer with the freezer program, and then I went
down to the Country Diner for lunch, and after that I
went to visit Ada Blount."

"That was nice of you. I know she always appreciates
company. But don't you think you'd better get moving if
you're going to get ready?"

"Ready? For what?" Kate frantically racked her brain
but drew a blank.

"It's Friday night. The dinner dance down at the
Depot Inn? The annual fund-raiser for community projects," Paul reminded her. He looked surprised that she'd
forget a social occasion like this. "That's why I took a
shower early, to give you a chance to get all prettied up."

"Oh good heavens!" Kate exclaimed, leaping away from him. "Look at the time."

"You've got an hour and a half."

"That's barely enough," she called as she ran to their bedroom.

Paul followed, slowly, rubbing his head with the towel. "You must have had quite a day."

Kate whirled around the bedroom, pulling out underwear and stockings from the dresser and laying them on the bed. "Yes, well, all kinds of things happened."

"Such as?"

"Well, first off, Joe Tucker dropped a pan of lasagna all over himself and the kitchen floor," Kate said, her voice muffled as she looked in the closet for the shoes she'd bought to go with her new dress. "But it wasn't his fault. Kisses attacked him."

Paul laughed. "Kisses attacked Joe? What did he go for, his toes?"

"He was going for the lasagna," Kate said, emerging with a shoe box that contained a pair of cream-colored wedges. "He was in Renee's tote in the corner, and when Joe opened the oven door, Kisses burst out."

"I'll bet that was a sight."

"It was." Kate set the shoe box down beside the bed. "Did you leave me any hot water?"

"I think so," Paul said.

Kate started to pass him on her way to the bathroom, but he pulled her into his arms. "So, what are you wearing tonight?"

"It's a surprise. Now let me get ready and do you proud, Mr. Hanlon."

"You always do." He grinned.

She kissed him lightly on the cheek and hurried to the bathroom.

As she showered and dressed, Kate wondered why she hadn't told Paul everything. She wasn't sure. For one thing, she didn't want to put a damper on such a special evening. For another, there really wasn't time to fill him in beforehand. Besides, it would upset Paul terribly and she really didn't have any hard facts yet. *But those are all excuses*, she thought. *The truth is, I'm not ready to talk about this with anybody, even Paul.*

Kate finished brushing her hair and twisted it up into a knot, leaving little wisps to frame her face. She put on a touch of lipstick and powder, then went out into the living room. Paul was sitting on the couch, reading a book. He glanced up as she came in, rose, and took a long, careful look at her. She was wearing an embroidered pink jacquard jacket over a bias-cut cream-chiffon dress. The pink set off her skin; the chiffon skirt swirled gently around her legs. Her warm brown eyes glowed as he smiled.

"I'm such a lucky man. You look absolutely beautiful," he said, his blue eyes shining with pride.

"Thank you," she replied, taking his arm. "I'm pretty lucky myself."

"Flattery will get you everywhere," he smiled, kissing her.

Kate laughed. "I'm so glad we're together," she whispered as they went to the car.

THE DINNER DANCE was being held at the Depot Inn on Main Street for two reasons: It was convenient and it was traditional. Some people, specifically Renee Lambert, had argued that it was time to move the annual fund-raiser to the Hamilton Springs Hotel, with its lavish ballroom and world-class restaurant, but she had been ignored. Some things were just too hard to change.

The large banquet room was decorated with pink and white crepe-paper ribbons and streamers, pink and white balloons, and a massive bouquet of pink and white flowers that stood on a small table in front of the podium. Nobody was at the podium and the band wasn't playing yet, which was just as well. With almost everyone in town there, talking and laughing, the noise was deafening.

Kate looked around as Paul took their coats and hung them up. Livvy Jenner and her husband, Danny, were across the room talking to Sam Gorman, owner of the Mercantile. Kate could see Amanda Bly with Dot Bagley, Martha Sinclair, and a group of elderly ladies already seated at one of the round dining tables, all talking animatedly. Joe Tucker and Skip Spencer, the town deputy, were talking intently about something, which was surprising, considering the vast age difference between them. But then, Joe found something interesting to talk about with everyone he met.

Kate and Paul worked their way across the room toward the Jenners, with whom they were to share a table.

"Kate!" Livvy said. "You look lovely! And so elegant. Talbots?"

"Yes," Kate said. "I couldn't resist. I love your outfit too."

"Thanks," Livvy said. She was wearing a beaded black tunic over a black sheath. As they all sat down, she added, "I got it last Christmas and this is the first chance I've had to wear it. Say, I thought you were going to stop by the library earlier. I was hoping we could go for a walk."

"I'm sorry. I was working at Faith Freezer this morning," Kate said, gazing around the table. Each place was already set with water, rolls and salad.

"Maybe next week. We've got to get out and enjoy this beautiful weather."

"I know," Kate agreed and then looked around the room. "It's a great turnout, isn't it?"

"A little loud," Livvy said, sighing.

"Everything okay?" Kate asked.

"Oh yes. It's just that we had all the sixth graders over at the library this afternoon for a workshop on pirates." Livvy shook her head. "They enjoyed themselves heartily and I still have a slight headache."

"So much for quiet in the library?"

Livvy rolled her eyes. "Those days are long gone," she said. "When I think back to when I was a little girl, you never dreamed of making a sound. But now the children run around, making all the noise they can, and when you ask the mothers or the teachers if they could be a little quieter, you just get a look like you'd asked them to stuff the kids into a closet."

Kate tried not to giggle.

"Tell me about your latest stained-glass project," Livvy prompted.

"Well, I've got an idea for night-light covers," Kate said. "Roses. Red, white, pink, and maybe blue. What do you think?"

"I think they sound lovely. When can I see one?"

"Well, I haven't actually made one yet . . . just sketches," Kate admitted. "But as soon as I do, I'll bring one down for you to look at."

The entrées were being served and Paul said a quiet grace for their table. As they ate fried chicken, mashed potatoes, fried okra, and green beans, the group chatted about events around town.

"Say," Danny said, "have you guys seen the little 1971 Roadster MG the Wilson boys are restoring?"

"No!" Sam and Paul said simultaneously, with identical longing.

"It's the prettiest thing you ever saw in your life," Danny went on. "Cherry red, with—"

Livvy leaned over to Kate and said, "We've lost them for the evening."

Kate nodded. "I'm afraid so."

The men went from talking about the MG to LuAnne Matthews' new truck, and the discussion lasted through the chess pie and coffee. It only stopped when Lawton Briddle, mayor of Copper Mill, rose and went to the podium. The microphone gave a long squeal, crackled, and then settled down as Lawton spoke, welcoming everyone and thanking folks for coming.

"Now y'all know that this community fund-raiser is a fairly recent part of Copper Mill history. It got started during

World War II as a savings-bond drive for the war effort.
Back then our chairwoman was Caroline Beauregard
Johnston, who chaired it for many, many years, and we are
all very thankful to her."

The mayor continued, "After the war was over, everyone agreed that it would be a shame to let such a fun community event come to an end."

Everyone applauded.

"And now we use the funds for various community
projects around town. Over the years the fund-raiser has
paid for everything from the cenotaph in the cemetery,
memorializing Copper Mill's war dead, to the Arbor Day
plantings in the various parks around town. In the past ten
years, it's helped fund the Girl Scouts, the Regional Early
Childhood Intervention Program, the County Help Line,
the County Crisis Center, the Reading and Radio
Resource, and our latest members, the Bixby House
Temporary Shelter and Faith Freezer Program."

Kate winced.

Lawton raised his hands and said, "Let's all give a
round of applause to all of these worthy programs."

As she joined in the applause, Kate again thought of
her conversation with Emma and said a quick prayer that
everything would turn out all right.

"Well, folks, enough of my talk. Let's have a big hand
for everyone involved in this event. Loretta Sweet, food.
Sam Gorman, publicity. Abby Pippins, decorations. And,
of course, Renee Lambert, our chairwoman."

Everyone stood as their names were called and Renee

was still standing when the applause stopped. She sat down as Lawton finished his speech, "And now, let's work off some of that wonderful dinner with dancing and music from Jack Kelly's Small Town Big Band Orchestra!"

There was more applause as Lawton stepped away from the microphone with a flourish and the music started.

Paul looked across at Kate and asked, "Would you care to dance, Mrs. Hanlon?"

"I'd love to, Mr. Hanlon." She smiled at him as he walked around the table and took her hand. He led her to the dance floor and they began to sway.

"This is so nice," Kate said after a few minutes.

"I agree. It reminds me of when we were courting."

She smiled again and nestled closer to him. There were a number of couples on the dance floor, including Junius and Amanda. Renee was dancing with Lawton Briddle, and the Jenners were on the floor as well. Joe was sitting at a table next to the dance floor, his eyes following Amanda wherever Junius took her.

I do believe he has a crush on her, Kate thought. *Well, they say opposites attract, but . . . poor man. I don't think he has a chance.*

Sitting beside Joe were Old Man Parsons and Clifton Beasley, both ignoring the dancing as they worked their way through the extra pieces of pie at their table. As Paul guided her around the floor, Kate saw Matt Lawson standing alone near the coffee urns.

He looks like a long-tailed cat in a room full of rockers, Kate thought. *Why does he come to these things if all he's going to do is stand in a corner?* Suddenly the idea of Matt being a crook seemed absolutely ludicrous. He didn't seem capable of it. For that matter, she didn't even know if he'd ever been to Ada's. That was something she'd have to check out.

"Oh, I'm so sorry!" Renee's voice boomed out.

Kate glanced over and saw that Renee was speaking to Amanda.

"I was being whirled around so that I never noticed where we were going."

"It's my fault," Lawton said.

"I should say it was," Renee chided playfully. "But never mind. We'll just keep going. I could dance all night."

Kate raised her eyebrows at Paul, who smiled back. The music stopped and everyone clapped. "Do you feel like dancing all night?" Paul asked.

"After some more coffee," Kate said.

They threaded their way back to their table. Sam had gone over to Joe's table and they were talking with animation. Even Old Man Parsons seemed to be interested, so Kate decided they weren't discussing the MG or the truck. Old Man Parsons didn't care about cars or any other form of modern technology.

As the evening progressed, Kate's main entertainment, apart from dancing with Paul and chatting with Livvy, was watching Renee Lambert chasing Junius Lawson. LuAnne had been right: Junius was popular. Over the next two hours, he danced with almost every lady there except Renee and it was obviously disturbing her. Especially when he asked Amanda to dance a second time. Amanda refused, but she must have done it very nicely, Kate thought, because Junius' feelings didn't seem to be hurt. He moved on to Dot Bagley, and when their dance was over, he came by the Hanlon table.

"Kate," he said, "would you dance with me?"

"Aren't you tired yet, Junius?" Kate asked, laughing. "You've danced with almost everyone in the room."

"But not you," he pointed out. "Would you?"

"I'd love to," Kate said.

As they spun around the dance floor, Kate realized she was in the hands of a master. She felt more graceful, more light on her feet than she ever had before. Junius was such a wonderful dancer that he made her look—and feel—much better than she was.

"You're a wonderful dancer," Junius said when the music stopped.

"No," Kate said honestly. "You are. And you make who-ever dances with you wonderful."

Junius' cheeks reddened. "Well, everyone has a talent. I've always loved to dance."

"You should have gone to Hollywood," Kate said.

"Given Fred Astaire a run for his money?"

"Of course."

Junius shook his head. "No. Asheville was a big enough town for me."

"Is that where you're from?"

"Lived there for years. It's a great city."

"A lot bigger than Copper Mill," Kate said.

"*Mmm.* But I've grown to love it here. A small town is a warm place to be, especially as you grow old. Not that you'd know about that," Junius added, his eyes twinkling.

"You are a flatterer," Kate said.

Junius smiled widely. "Not at all. Another dance sometime?"

"I would be more than happy to," Kate replied.

He bowed, then went off in search of another partner.

"Well!" Renee's voice boomed as she came up beside Kate. "I don't know what other people think, but in the old days, pastors' wives didn't dance with anyone but their husbands. If they danced at all!"

Kate paused so she wouldn't say something she'd regret. Then she smiled brightly. "You're right. I'll have to remember that. Now, if you'll excuse me. I've got to go talk to someone." And before Renee could say anything else, Kate walked over to Amanda's table. "Hello, Amanda. May I sit with you awhile?"

"Please do," Amanda said.

Kate sat down and looked across the room. Sure enough, there went Renee, positioning herself to be next in line to dance with Junius.

"So, how are you enjoying the evening?" Kate asked.

"Very much," Amanda replied. "We don't have a lot of occasions like these anymore in Copper Mill."

"Did there used to be more? When you were young?" Kate knew Amanda had grown up in Copper Mill and would know all about the town's history.

"Oh yes. There weren't all these videos and disks and

things. We had to make our own entertainment, so we had hay rides and barn dances and street dances and every kind of dance we could get away with." Amanda's eyes were bright. "It was wonderful. I feel sorry for young girls today. They don't ever dress up, it seems, and they don't ever get to dance cheek to cheek, and they don't seem nearly as happy as we were. But then maybe I'm just being nostalgic."

Kate nodded.

"Probably everybody feels their youth, the time they were young, was the best, simply because it was theirs," Amanda continued. "Just as when you're young, you know that nobody ever felt as strongly, thought as deeply, or lived as fully as you do." She smiled a little ruefully. "No wonder there's always a generation gap. Robert Browning had it right when he wrote 'Grow old along with me! The best is yet to be.'"

Kate smiled, delighted, and Amanda recited some more of the poem. Then she stopped and sighed.

Kate glanced over to where Paul was talking with Joe, Sam, and Skip. The four looked as if they were all talking at once, happy and excited. She sincerely hoped that she and Paul would grow old together, that their thirty years of marriage would become forty, fifty, even sixty. *As many years as possible, please, Lord.*

"I hope Joe isn't leading those boys into trouble," Amanda said sharply, looking at the group huddled around him.

"What on earth do you mean?" Kate asked, surprised.

"Just that when I was a girl, if there was any misbehavior going on, Joe Tucker was always in the thick of it."

Kate looked at Amanda in disbelief.

Dot Bagley came over, carrying coats. "You about ready to go, Amanda?"

"Yes, I think so," Amanda said, getting up carefully and putting on her coat. "I'm tired."

"Wait a minute," Kate said anxiously. "What you said about Joe . . ."

Amanda sighed. "All that was a long time ago. I shouldn't have said anything. Forget what I said, please?"

Kate assured Amanda she would, but after a minute, she got up and walked over to Paul's group, passing Renee, who was smiling broadly as she danced with Junius.

The four men stopped talking as soon as Kate approached, and the look on Paul's face made her ask as lightly as she could, "What are y'all plotting over here, anyway?"

"Wh-wh-what?" Paul stuttered.

"She's caught us, gentlemen," Joe said. "We're going to have to tell her the truth." He turned to Kate, leaned forward on his walking stick, and said solemnly, "These boys were making plans to take over the government and institute a new world order. Everybody's going to have to sleep late in the morning, eat dessert first, and go fishing every Saturday. What do you think?"

"I think you look a little guilty for something as silly as that," Kate replied, her eyes on Paul. He *did* look guilty. What was going on?

Joe shook his head. "Now isn't that a woman for you? Always trying to find out a man's secrets and never willing to share hers."

"True." She managed a smile. "But I'm always pre-pared to listen."

Joe laughed. "You are one determined lady. I'll leave her to you, Pastor," he said and walked off, taking Skip with him.

Kate turned to Paul. "Is there something I should know?" she asked seriously.

"No," Paul replied. "We were just cooking up a little plan for the summer concert series."

"Oh, the root-beer floats," Kate said, feeling a surpris-ing amount of relief. "Joe told us all about that at lunch."

Paul and Sam exchanged a quick glance.

"Did he? Well, he's got a few more ideas like that," Sam said.

Suddenly Kate found herself yawning.

"You're tired," Paul said. "Let's go home. See you later, Sam."

"Later, Paul."

Kate and Paul headed toward the door. Most people were gone. Renee and Junius were still dancing, almost alone on the dance floor. Maybe Renee would get to dance all night.

Kate looked up at Paul and snuggled closer to him. *"Grow old along with me! The best is yet to be."*

Chapter Four

K ate awoke before dawn Monday morning and lay in the half light, listening to the birds calling the sun to rise. Paul breathed softly beside her, his hair tousled and a slight smile on his face.

Kate smiled, her heart flooded with tenderness. Their son, Andrew, was the spitting image of his father, and looking at Paul now reminded her of all the times when she'd gotten Andrew up and ready for school. How he'd hated it! Now, she knew, he often got up at four in the morning to go for a run before heading to work as a real-estate lawyer in Philadelphia. She chuckled softly and then glanced again at Paul, worried that she'd disturbed him. Quiet as a mouse, she crept out of bed.

A few minutes later, she padded softly into the kitchen and got the coffeepot going, making as little sound as possible. Then she sat in her rocking chair for her usual early morning time with God. The sun would be up in a few minutes, the birds were still chirping their hearts out, and there was a faint mist all along the ground in the backyard, swirling around the trees.

Kate opened her devotional book and read the Bible passage for the day: Proverbs 31:10–31. "*A wife of noble character who can find? She is worth far more than rubies. Her husband has full confidence in her and lacks nothing of value. She brings him good, not harm, all the days of her life ...*" She thought of Paul and her mind raced back over all their years together, memory upon memory, from when they first met—how young they had been!—to now, with Paul, tousled hair and all, asleep in the bedroom. He had brought her nothing but good all the days of her life. She hoped she had done the same for him. *She gets up while it is still dark ...* That was certainly true.

When the coffee was ready, Kate got up and poured herself a cup, looking out the kitchen window. This was the time of day she loved best, with the sun just breaking over the mountains. She settled back into her rocker and read some more. When she got to verse 26, "*She speaks with wisdom, and faithful instruction is on her tongue ...,*" Ada Blount leaped into her mind. For a moment, panic washed over her. Then Kate bent her head and prayed with all her heart for Ada, Emma, and everyone involved in the Faith Freezer Program, including herself. *Lord, please, please help me speak with wisdom today.*

When she had finished praying, Kate got up and did what she always did when she needed to sort her thoughts out: She turned on the oven and started baking.

"THOSE WERE DELICIOUS," Paul said, finishing a fresh-baked apple-bran muffin.

"And they were good for you," Kate responded, smiling.

"Which is the only reason you let me have three of them," he retorted.

"That's right," Kate said. "I'm determined to keep you fit and healthy."

"You do a wonderful job."

She leaned over and kissed him. "Yes, as long as I can keep an eye on you. I know you sneak down to the Smokeshack and have ribs every chance you get."

"Look at it as my way of helping the local economy thrive." He finished the last of his coffee in his "World's Best Preacher" mug and got up. "Well, I'd better get down to the church. Are you going to get a chance to work in your studio today?"

Kate sighed. "I don't know. I have a couple of errands to run. It depends on how long they take."

"And on who you meet. I know how easy it is to get sidetracked in this town." Paul smiled at her, his clear blue eyes twinkling. "I'm glad you went to visit Ada last week. How is she doing?"

"Oh well. She thought I was someone named Marybeth at first. I think that was her first cousin. I'm not sure . . . But eventually she realized who I was."

"Poor woman. And poor Emma." Paul's face clouded. "It's hard to see someone you love slipping away like that. And sadly, it's only going to get worse. But God is still with her, still loves her, no matter what."

"Amen." Kate looked over at the clock. "You'd better get a move on or Millie will be nagging you again. 'Pastor Hanlon's a wonderful man, but he's always running late. I've told him and told him, but there it is,'" Kate said, mimicking the faithful church secretary.

Paul grimaced. "You're almost too good at that. See you tonight, sweetheart," he said, kissing her good-bye.

"Don't be late," Kate called. "I'm making pork chops."

"Wouldn't miss it," Paul called back and went out the door to the garage.

Kate watched his blue Chevy pickup pull out of the garage and go down the road. Then she washed and dried the dishes, made the bed, put away the clothes Paul had left strewn around, and threw some towels in the washing machine, hoping she'd remember to put them in the dryer when she got back from her errands. Then she combed her hair and put on a dab of lipstick. She was wearing a white shirt and sage green twill pants, and she chose a rose-colored cotton cardigan to go with it, tying a light silk floral scarf around her neck for warmth. Later it would be warm enough that she wouldn't need the sweater or the scarf, but Copper Mill was in the mountains and even in summer the air could be cool in the early part of the day. At least it felt cool to a Texas girl.

Kate got in her black Honda Accord and backed out of the garage. She needed to stop at the Mercantile and see if she could find some red peppers to bake with feta cheese as a side dish. She also needed to get gas, and she really wanted to go talk to Matt Lawson. She already knew

which was going to be last on her list. As she approached
the Bixby house, she saw Livvy's car in the driveway. Kate
had planned to stop by the house later, but since she was
there, she decided to stop and talk to her friend.

Walking into the kitchen gave Kate a profound sense
of déjà vu: There was Renee, leaning against the counter,
Kisses in Renee's tote in the corner, and Joe standing at
the sink, washing his hands. But today Livvy was helping,
the meals were already packed, and Amanda Bly, Martha
Sinclair, and Betty Anderson, the proprietor of Betty's
Beauty Parlor, were piling them into boxes.

"Kate!" Livvy called out. "I didn't know you were helping today."

"Oh, I'm not. I just thought I'd pop in and see how
everything's going."

Renee called out, "Well, I can tell you that *some* people were complaining about getting shorted on the lasagna
Friday."

"Well, they're not getting shorted today," Livvy said.
"Turkey sandwiches and chicken soup."

"Now that don't make sense," Joe Tucker said. "Why
two fowls at one meal? And why not the same fowl?
Chicken sandwiches and chicken soup, or turkey sandwiches and turkey soup. Why kill two birds for one meal?"

Renee gave him a look of amazement that was almost
admiration. "It takes a special kind of mind to think of
something like that," she said. "Well, I've got to get going.
I promised to take Mama for a little drive." She picked up
her bag and held Kisses up to her face. "How's my Little

Umpkins? Is my Little Umpkins hungry?" Then she looked up quickly. "Bridge this afternoon, Martha!"

"I know," Martha replied. "At Agnes Kelly's."

"Bring canapés," Renee reminded her, then left.

"You know," Betty said, looking at Amanda's hair, "I was thinking that a blue rinse would really set off your coloring. And maybe just a little shorter haircut?"

"She'd look like everybody else if you did that," Martha exclaimed without thinking, as usual. Then she flushed and said, "Well, I mean that French knot is just so stylish."

"If it was pink," Joe said, surprising all of them, "it'd be like cotton candy." Then he turned away and started piling dirty dishes in the sink as everyone stared at him.

"Thanks for the idea," Amanda said, determinedly not looking at Joe. "But I've worn it this way for years and I think I'll keep it."

"Oh, and it looks lovely," Betty assured her. "I was just thinking that it would be so much easier to take care of . . . By the way," she said, quickly changing the subject, "has anyone seen a ring? A small silver ring, set with turquoise? I can't find it anywhere and the last time I saw it was when I was working here last week. I took it off while I was washing the dishes."

"I haven't seen anything like that," Amanda said.

"Nor me," Joe said.

"Me neither," said Martha.

"Nor have I," Kate added, hoping her face didn't betray the concern she felt. "But we'll all keep an eye out for it."

"Thanks," Betty said. "It's not very valuable, but it's a pretty little thing and I like it. Here, Amanda, I'll take that out for you."

"Thank you, dear," Amanda said.

"Come by my place for some coffee after," Martha urged Amanda as they walked out.

"That sounds lovely," Amanda said.

Joe watched them go, his eyes fixed on Amanda. Kate and Livvy exchanged a glance.

"Well," he said, turning back to the sink, "I reckon we'd best get on with the washing up."

"Oh, don't worry about it, Joe," Livvy said. "You go on home and I'll clean up."

"I feel guilty, always leaving the cleaning to someone else," he replied. "I did KP in the army, same as everyone else, and I wash my own dishes at home, you know."

"I'm sure you did. But there's nothing to this. Go on," Livvy urged.

"Okay, you win," Joe said, holding his hands up in surrender. He winked, picked up his walking stick, and walked toward the door before he could get suckered back into helping.

"Knowing Joe, he's probably off to read *War and Peace* or something." Livvy laughed at Kate's incredulous look. "Joe plays the hillbilly well, but believe me, he's one of the best-read men in Copper Mill. He's in the library almost every day, and he's not just there for the newspapers or the heat in winter. I've often wondered what he does with all that information. I guess he just likes to learn."

Kate nodded. *"Mmm."*

Livvy looked across at her friend and said, *"Mm-hmm.*
What's going on?"

"What do you mean?"

"I know you, Kate Hanlon. And I saw your face when
Betty asked about her ring. Something's going on. That's
why I got Joe out of here. What is it?"

Kate sighed. "Can we have a cup of coffee?"

"Sure. Sit down and I'll serve some right up."

Kate sat down and pulled off her sweater and scarf as
Livvy heated two cups of coffee in the microwave.

"Now, tell me," she said, setting a steaming mug in
front of Kate.

Kate took a deep breath and told Livvy everything.

"And now, with Betty missing a ring, I can't help but
think maybe there *is* a thief among us," Kate concluded.

Livvy shook her head. "I can't believe that. The money's
serious, I agree. But the rest of it . . . I don't know. People
lose things all the time. It could all just be coincidence.
And you know how it is when one thing piles up on top of
another; it's hard not to see it as something more sinister."

"But what if it is something sinister?" Kate asked.

"Well, one thing I do know. Joe Tucker would never be
guilty of anything like that. He's been an upstanding
member of this community for fifty years. So that's one
volunteer in the Faith Freezer Program who's in the clear,"
Livvy assured Kate, who nodded. "I'll ask around about
who's missing what. It'll be a good excuse to get away from
James's band rehearsing for the summer concert series. "

"James is playing?" Kate took a sip of her coffee, imagining Livvy's teenage son onstage.

"He's in a garage band." Livvy rolled her eyes and sighed. "Bring earplugs. They're not bad; just loud. And Danny is going to emcee. It's a huge deal around here. Everyone participates. Even Old Man Parsons tells stories."

"He does?"

"Old-timey ones. The kids love it. And there are bands and choral groups and duets and all kinds of stuff. Basically, everyone in town is there, either playing, singing, or applauding wildly."

"Ah," Kate said, raising her hand. "That will be my contribution. Wild applause."

"Are you sure you don't want to participate? I know there are a couple of groups . . ." Livvy eyed Kate thoughtfully.

"No," Kate said firmly.

Livvy laughed. "All right. But keep it in mind."

"I will," Kate said blandly. She looked at her watch. "Well, I've got to get going. I have so many things to do today."

"And I've got to get back to the library." Livvy looked around at the soup pot, ladle, and other cooking utensils still waiting to be washed and dried and put away. "Oh dear."

"Don't worry about them," Kate said. "I'll take care of it."

"Are you sure?"

Kate nodded.

Livvy reached over and gave Kate a quick hug. "Thank you. It's all going to work out fine, you know."

"I hope so," Kate sighed. "Say a prayer."

"I will," Livvy said.

Kate cleaned up the kitchen as quickly as possible, then headed into town to take care of her errands.

THE BANK, officially the Mid-Cumberland Bank and Trust, Copper Mill Branch, was an imposing brick building with long narrow windows and large plate-glass doors that looked out on the Town Square. Since it was over a hundred years old, Kate always walked in expecting it to smell of old, dry books and furniture polish, but as always the dominating scent was that of rich, freshly brewed coffee. As she stopped at the little cart by the front doors and helped herself to a cup from the urn, she raised herself up on tiptoe but couldn't see over the three-quarter cubicle walls that surrounded the offices of the bank manager, Melvin McKinney, and Matt Lawson.

The fact that Mr. McKinney hadn't come running out to greet her was proof that he was either busy with a client or out. As for Matt, she'd find out about him in a minute. Evelyn or Georgia Cline, the elderly twins who had been tellers at the bank since the dawn of time, would fill her in. She walked over to the tellers' windows and Georgia spotted her first.

"Mrs. Hanlon!" she called out. "What can I do for you today?"

"Just a small deposit," Kate said, pulling out the check

she'd received from a stained-glass order for a sun catcher. "How are you doing today?"

"Just fine," Georgia said, processing the deposit. "Evelyn's got a bit of a cold, but I'm making her gargle with hot salt water. That should fix her up."

Kate suppressed a shudder.

Evelyn, whose red nose seemed even brighter against her white skin and blue-rinsed hair, scooted her stool over and said in a hoarse voice, "It's not doing much good so far."

"Well, that's because you're not doing it often enough." Georgia sighed and handed Kate her receipt. "I swear, these young'uns."

Kate raised an eyebrow.

"Evelyn's five minutes younger than I am, but you'd think it was five years, considering how she carries on sometimes. So what's new?"

"How about LuAnne Matthews' truck," Evelyn croaked. "Isn't that something?"

"It is nice," Kate said. "Are you thinking of buying a new car?"

"Not hardly," Georgia replied.

Evelyn said scratchily, "It's just that she didn't finance it through us—"

Kate knew that by "us," Evelyn meant the bank.

"Evelyn!" Georgia snapped. "That's nobody's business but hers."

Evelyn ducked back to her side of the teller's counter. "Sorry about that."

Kate thought swiftly. These two women knew almost everything that went on in town and they obviously seemed to know about any unusual financial transactions. So she decided to take a risk. "Does either of you know anything about someone who was going around town this winter—"

"A stranger?" Evelyn interrupted, gasping.

"I'm not sure," Kate said. "He was running some sort of investment scam and some people gave him money. Not cash, but checks written to cash. Large checks."

"How large?" Georgia asked.

"A few thousand," Kate said, watching their faces carefully.

Georgia shook her head. "Nothing like that crossed this counter." She glanced at Evelyn, who shook her head.

"Nobody around here's written a check to cash for more than fifty dollars. Well, maybe a hundred. And I haven't seen any strangers, either," Georgia said regretfully.

"Well, it was just a rumor. You know how those things get started. By the way," Kate said lightly, hoping it sounded like she didn't care all that much, "is Mr. Lawson in?"

"Oh, he's back there . . . Don't you dare sneeze all over me!"

Kate jumped, but then realized that Georgia was talking to her sister.

"No one's with him," Georgia said, turning back to Kate.

"He's originally from Asheville, North Carolina, isn't he?" Kate asked. "I was talking to his father Friday night."

"Junius?" Evelyn asked.

Kate nodded.

"Such a wonderful man," she croaked. "And what a good dancer!"

"And such a conversationalist," Georgia added. Then she lowered her voice and said, "He must be so disappointed in his son."

Kate looked at her quizzically.

"About as interesting as watching paint dry. But they do say he's good at what he does." Georgia shrugged. "Hard to believe, considering."

"Considering what?" Kate asked, hoping God would forgive this wholesale dive into gossip.

"Well," Evelyn chimed in with a hoarse whisper, "he had his own investment firm in Asheville, and somehow or other it went belly-up."

"But he's doing well here," Georgia added.

"That's good to know," Kate said. "Would it be okay if I went back to see him for a minute?"

"You go right on back, Mrs. Hanlon," Georgia said. "He's not doing a thing he can't stop for a minute."

"Thank you," Kate said and walked back to the office.

Matt's door was open and he was sitting straight up at his desk, looking at his laptop. His face looked more alert, more interested than Kate had ever seen it, she thought as she knocked on the doorjamb. She had to knock twice before he looked up. His face lost all its animation the minute he saw her.

"Matt? Could I speak to you for a few minutes?" Kate asked.

"Oh, of course," he said without standing up.

He was wearing a brown suit with a white shirt and a beige tie. Kate had noticed that his outfits were always monochromatic.

"Come in."

Kate walked in and shut the door behind her.

"How can I help you?" he asked as she sat down. "Investment questions?"

"In a way," Kate said. She was holding her purse tightly on her lap and she made herself set it down on the floor beside her. "I was visiting with Ada Blount on Friday and she mentioned that someone has been stopping by talking investments with her—something about doubling her money."

Matt didn't say anything. He didn't react. Instead, he simply looked not at Kate but at a point somewhere to one side of her head. Silence hung in the air like a dark cloud. Kate finally took a deep breath and continued, "Was it you?"

There was another shorter silence, then Matt asked, with almost no curiosity in his voice, "Did I specifically advise her?"

"Yes," Kate replied, then waited.

Matt nodded. He thought for a moment and then said, "I don't know anything about any investments Mrs. Blount might have made. But . . ."

The pause was so long, Kate couldn't stand it. "But you've spoken to her about such matters?" she asked. His blank face made it impossible for her to guess what he was really thinking or feeling.

"Of course," Matt replied. "I talk about investments with everyone. It's my area of expertise, advising people regarding their assets and making suggestions for their future."

"So you've been advising and making suggestions to everyone you deliver meals to?"

"Of course," Matt said, his face showing an expression for the first time: faint surprise. There was another long pause, then he asked, "Did something happen with Mrs. Blount?"

"I'm not in a position to say," Kate replied.

Matt thought for a moment, then said, "I did talk with Mrs. Blount, but I can assure you that I know nothing at all about her investments and I never received any funds from her. And I assure you that in the future, I won't discuss investments with any Faith Freezer client outside of my own office. Is that what you wanted?"

"Yes." Kate sighed. What else could she say? She picked up her purse. "You will keep our conversation confidential?" she asked. "I wouldn't want people to—"

"Anything discussed in this office is automatically confidential." He said it as a statement of fact, not an assurance.

"Thank you."

Matt nodded. "If I can ever help you and Pastor Hanlon with any of your financial arrangements, please let me know. Here's my card."

Kate took the business card, puzzled and frustrated. She walked past the teller's counter, waving good-bye to the Cline sisters, and went outside, where she took a long, deep breath. What was it about Matt that always left her feeling as if she had literally been talking to a brick wall? His stolidity, for one. That immobile face. All the little expressions that flitted across most people's faces didn't flit across his.

Kate got into her car and drove to the gas station. As she was pumping gas, still thinking about Matt, it occurred to her for the first time that only half of any conversation was the actual words. The rest was in the gestures, the tilt of the eyebrows, the quirk of the lips . . . and Matt had none of those. Kate wondered whether he understood all those gestures and expressions in others. If not, he was missing the best part of any conversation he had. It would be like being color blind or tone deaf, only Kate thought this would be far more difficult to deal with.

She paid for her gas and went back downtown to shop for groceries at the Mercantile. Since Kate and Paul had moved to town, Sam Gorman, the owner, had taken to stocking more exotic groceries, like goat cheese and blue corn chips, and a wider array of fresh vegetables. She remembered how happy she'd been when he'd begun to carry puff pastry in the freezer and how many questions she'd had to answer about what to do with it.

She looked around the store for Sam, but he wasn't there. *Must be off having a cup of coffee at the diner*, she thought as she made her way to the produce section.

She was happy to find both leeks and red peppers. After years of ignoring leeks as simply fat scallions, Kate had finally tried a chicken-and-leek soup that had been so delicious, Paul had raved about it for days. After that, she'd been more experimental, and that evening for dinner, she was going to try a recipe for braised leeks with lemons and chicken broth. The leeks along with baked red peppers and feta cheese, pork chops, and some whole-wheat dinner rolls would make a lovely meal.

She bagged up the leeks and peppers, shivering slightly in the chilly air. *I should have brought my sweater.* The image of her sweater hooked on the back of a chair in the Bixby-house kitchen leaped into her mind.

Arlene Jacobs, the part-time cashier, rang up Kate's items, and Kate paid for her groceries. Then she returned to her car and headed back to the Bixby house to pick up her sweater.

As Kate got out of her car, she saw Martha Sinclair get in hers and drive off. At the same time, Junius came out the kitchen door. He saw her and shook his head.

"I wouldn't go in there if I were you," he said.

"Why not?" Kate asked.

Junius made a face. "Tell you the truth, bit of a cat fight."

Kate walked past him and opened the kitchen door.

"I don't know what you're talking about," Amanda Bly exclaimed when Kate entered.

"Oh, don't give me that," Renee snapped. "Looking like butter wouldn't melt in your mouth. You're nothing but a man-chasing flirt and you know it. You're just the same as you were back in high school. Miss Amanda, Miss Popularity, Miss Priss—"

"Don't tell me you're still mad about homecoming—"

"Homecoming! How dare you speak to me about homecoming?" Renee spat.

Kate was amazed to see tears in Renee's eyes and even more amazed to see Amanda blush fiery red.

"You *knew* about Charlie and me, and yet you stepped right in and—" Renee began.

"Ladies!" Kate interrupted, walking in between them. Both were quivering and flushed; Kate might have laughed if it wasn't so sad. "What on earth are you two fighting about?"

"I'm not fighting," Amanda managed to say, but Kate could see how upset she was. "Junius and I came by to drop off a box of containers—"

"And that's another thing," Renee launched forth again. "Who gave you a key to this place?"

"Martha let me in—"

"Yes, well, there's been some mighty funny things going on around here and no one is above suspicion." Renee snatched up her tote, giving Kisses such an awful jerk that he whimpered. "Now look. On top of everything else, you've got Kisses all upset."

She marched to the kitchen door and turned around. "A little more security around this place might not be a bad idea. And I can assure you, I'll be keeping an eye on you." Then she stomped out, slamming the door behind her.

The silence was deafening. "I'm so sorry," Kate finally said.

"So am I." Amanda looked as if she had a bad taste in

her mouth. Then Kate realized that she was trying not to cry.

"It's an old quarrel."

"I'm sorry," Kate repeated.

"Yes, well, no bones broken." Amanda managed to smile, but it was shaky. "It's just so . . . ridiculous. At our age!"

"Is it safe to come in now?" Junius poked his head through the door.

"Land sakes, yes," Amanda said.

"You ready for me to take you home?" he asked.

Amanda nodded. "I'll see you later, Kate."

"Take care," Kate replied.

With everyone gone, Kate took a deep breath. That scene had thoroughly upset her. She could only imagine what it had done to Amanda. To be railed at by a hysterical, obviously jealous woman. And, as Amanda had said, at their age. Kate sighed. *"Anger is cruel and fury overwhelming, but who can stand before jealousy?"*

Renee had been sweet on someone named Charlie, and Amanda had stolen him from her, or at least Renee believed she had. It was so long ago and yet the pain was still there, still unhealed. *"A wounded spirit who can bear?"* Poor Renee.

Kate picked up her sweater, still hooked on the back of the chair, and looked around for her silk scarf. It wasn't there. She looked in the sleeves of her sweater, on the chair, on the floor, on the countertops, in the corners, in the cabinets, even in the refrigerator. Her silk scarf was gone.

Chapter Five

Paul was in Joe Tucker's battered old Ford pickup, squeezed in between Joe and Sam Gorman. They were rattling down the winding country road that Barnhill Street became once it crossed the railroad tracks, heading to the Dew Drop Inn.

"What do you two think about Hank Williams?" Joe asked.

"I don't know any of his songs," Paul admitted.

Sam nodded agreement.

Joe shook his head. "What's the world coming to? Used to be *everybody* knew every Hank Williams song ever written."

"That was a bit before our time," Sam pointed out.

"I don't know about that," Joe said. "You should have learned a few of these back when we were roofing. I'd think you'd remember them."

"All I remember is how steep those roofs were and how scared I was about falling off," Sam said, chuckling.

Paul gave him a questioning look.

"I used to work with Joe back when I was in high school."

"Roofing business?" Paul asked.

"More than that," Joe said proudly. "Campbell's Construction would do anything you cared to have done. We could build a house, fix a house, side a house, roof a house. We built barns, bathrooms, sheds, closets. I remember building a gazebo once. Craziest idea I ever heard of. Why not just add on a porch? But it was pretty when it was done."

"I think every kid in town worked for them at one point or another," Sam said. "Eli Weston worked with us for a while before he took over the antique store."

Joe grinned. "Had to earn that date money somehow."

"Try college money. That's what put me through—working summers."

"I worked there until I ran out of gas when I hit my fifties." Joe turned the wheel to the right to avoid a pothole.

"There's also the little matter of falling off that roof," Sam pointed out.

"Yeah," Joe agreed. "Leg never did heal up properly. 'Course, what can you expect at that age? So I hung up my tool belt and retired. Good to get free of it," he said so stoutly that Paul didn't believe a word. "And, of course, I still do a little woodworking. Keep my hand in things that way."

Paul smiled as he watched the town go by through the

windshield and thought about what they were going to attempt. A bluegrass band! A ripple of excitement, tinged with anxiety, went through him. It had been years since he'd played any music at all, either as a hobby or with a group. A pastor didn't have much time for hobbies.

And now, here they were. Literally. Joe pulled into the rutted dirt parking lot outside the Dew Drop Inn. Paul got out of the truck, reached into the back, and pulled out a guitar case. He looked around with some trepidation. The old roadhouse was nothing but a wooden shack, its boards weathered gray and tacked all over with old signs, its windows pasted with ads for beer. The old, yellowed celluloid roadhouse sign was cracked and the screen door was askew on its hinges. Paul would have bet that the place hadn't been cleaned or painted since it was built.

"Come on, boys, here we are!" Joe called out, heading up the steps and into the building. The screen door slammed behind him.

"Doesn't look like much, does it?" Sam asked, holding his fiddle case against his chest.

Paul raised his eyebrows. His enthusiasm had just evaporated. He followed Sam up the creaking wood steps and blinked in the dim light indoors. A few wooden tables and chairs were set up in the open space before them. A long, heavy oak bar stretched across the left-hand side of the room, a row of stools beside it. The air smelled of stale beer, stale cigarettes, grease, and sawdust.

Paul was instantly transported back in time to when he was eighteen, just graduated from high school. He and some friends he'd been playing music with had gone down one Saturday night to the local roadhouse, more out of curiosity than anything else. They'd even had a few beers and tried to act as if they belonged there. But he hadn't. He'd been nauseated by much of what he heard, much of what he saw, and he'd been glad to leave. The next day he'd felt awful, with a headache and a queasy stomach, but that was nothing compared to what he'd felt when his father took him aside later and asked him what he'd been doing down at the Hitching Post. He'd stammered out some excuse, and he could still hear his father's response: "Paul, you're a man now and old enough to do what you please. But going down to a place like that is no way to prove it. I expect more of you than that." Now, in his sixties, Paul still felt the guilt flooding back.

"Hey, guys!" Skip Spencer came up to them, his red hair glowing in the murky atmosphere. He was off duty and looked even younger in street clothes than in his uniform. "Come check out the stage!"

The three threaded their way between the tables. Paul could see a couple of pool tables to the right, each one with a lit lamp above it that made the green fabric the most vivid color in the whole place.

What on earth am I doing here?

He knew the roadhouse's reputation for rowdiness. He could just imagine what people would say if word got out that he was spending time at the Dew Drop Inn. He shook his head, thinking that this was *not* a good idea for a pastor.

At the back was a small wooden stage, barely six feet wide by ten feet long. Joe was standing on it, talking with the largest man Paul had ever seen, both in height and girth.

"Sam, Paul!" Joe called out. "This here's Bo Twist. He runs the place."

They all exchanged greetings and shook hands.

"Nice to meet you, Pastor," said Bo. "Probably the only chance I'll get," he added.

"Well, you could always come to our church," Paul offered. "I'm there fairly often."

Bo shook his head. "I always sleep in on Sundays. Saturday's my busiest night. That's not to say I wouldn't come if I could. I don't have nothin' against God, which is more than some people can say."

Paul blinked. "Well, that's a start," he managed to say with a hint of a smile.

"So, you'uns gonna put together a bluegrass band. Sounds okay to me. I had some college kids wanted to practice out here a while back, but they played that rock music. I told them I can't take that stuff, not before night-fall. Tell you the truth, I can't even take it then, but my customers like it. Early in the morning, I need my quiet. You'uns want some coffee?"

"That'd be great, Bo," Joe said. "And can we get the stage lights turned on?"

"Sure," Bo said. "Light switch is right behind you."

He stumped off the stage, his weight making every heavy step send up a little squeak and a puff of dust from the floorboards.

Joe switched on the light and the four looked around. "Ain't this grand?" Joe asked.

"It sure is!" Skip agreed.

"I don't know," Paul said. "I'm not so sure this is a good idea. Isn't there anywhere else we can practice?"

"Don't worry," Joe said. "Nobody comes here during the day except a few old guys to drink coffee and reminisce about when they were young hotshots. I come out every once in a while for coffee and a hand of euchre with Old Man Parsons."

"Old Man Parsons?" Paul asked, astounded.

"Best euchre player in the county," Joe assured him. He put his arm around Paul. "It's okay. Trust me."

"Besides," Skip said with a grin, "it's got a stage!"

Paul made a bit of face but nodded.

"Let's get going!" Skip picked up his banjo and put the strap around his neck. Sam opened up his fiddle case and Paul pulled out his guitar. Joe sat down, cradling an instrument that looked like an accordion with strings.

"What on earth is that?" Skip asked.

"It's an Autoharp," Joe said. "Haven't you ever seen one before?"

"Well, maybe . . ." Skip looked doubtful. "What's it sound like?"

Joe ran his pick along the strings and Skip winced.

"Now don't get all frazzled," Joe said. "Listen to this." He started strumming and chording and then sang the opening verse of "Wildwood Flower." "You ever heard that?"

Skip nodded. He still looked doubtful, but that might

have been because of Joe's off-key voice. His playing wasn't too bad.

"You sure don't look like Mother Maybelle," Bo said, coming up with a pot of coffee in one hand and a stack of Styrofoam cups in the other.

"I look more like her than you do," Joe replied, laughing.

"Got me there. Here you go, boys." Everyone took a cup and he filled them. "So, whatcha gonna call this here band?"

"We haven't gotten that far," Sam said.

"I was thinking we should call ourselves the Copper Mill Players," Skip suggested. "There aren't any other groups out there with that name and that way we're unique right from the start. And that's important. All the professionals say you've got to make your mark right from the beginning. Right name, right attitude, right set. Always make sure you're playing stuff people know and like, and then later you can work in some new pieces."

"You writing music now?" Joe asked.

Skip flushed. "I might be thinking about it. Anyway, after our debut down at the summer concert series on the Town Green, I was thinking we could go around the bluegrass festivals, maybe even get to the Smoky Mountain Fiddlers Convention. I'll tell you what, you get known there, you've got a real shot at something. Maybe even end up in Nashville. And before you know it, you're on your way!" he finished raptly, his eyes glowing with hope.

Bo looked over at Joe and said, "This boy's got some plans, don't he?"

Joe nodded. "Every young'un's got plans. You know that. And most of them center around some pretty girl. It'd probably save us a lot of time if you'd just tell us her name, Skip."

Skip flushed again. "I just think we should take this seriously. You never know. We might really have a future."

"Okay," Joe said. "We'll find out soon enough." He looked over at Sam and Paul, winking. "You boys ready?"

Sam picked up his fiddle and bow; Paul his guitar.

Joe nodded. "Better get tuned up together first, then we'll see what we can do."

It was hard to get all tuned together. Paul's ear told him that they still weren't right when Joe said, "Well, we might as well just get going."

"So what do we play?" Sam asked.

"I know some stuff by Kentucky Thunder," Skip said.

"I don't," Joe said. "How about 'Jambalaya'?"

"That's not bluegrass," Sam pointed out.

"How about 'Restless'?" Skip suggested.

"I don't know that one," Joe replied.

"This is crazy!" Sam said. "Isn't there anything we all know?"

"How about 'I'll Fly Away'?" Paul said. The four men looked at each other and everybody nodded.

"Let's try it," Joe said. "And a one and a two . . ."

Skip started out with the melody on banjo. Joe strummed his Autoharp, but it didn't fit with the banjo, and his face had a puzzled, lost look. Sam's fiddling was unsteady, the notes dragging just a little too long. First

Paul couldn't remember what chords to use and then he seemed to have lost some of his knack for fingering.

Finally Joe quit playing the Autoharp and started singing, and everyone joined in. Badly. The worst was when they got to the refrain. The high notes were too high for anybody but Skip.

Paul stopped and waved his hands. After a minute, everyone else was quiet.

"Look, guys, this isn't working. Not this way." Paul sighed. "Maybe if we had music."

"You mean sheet music?" Joe asked.

Paul nodded.

"I can't read music," Joe said. "I've always just strummed it out by ear."

That might account for it, Paul thought.

"I brought some sheet music," Skip offered. "I've got music for the soundtrack of that movie *O Brother, Where Art Thou?*"

"Well, why didn't you say so earlier?" Joe asked.

Skip looked a little sheepish. "I thought maybe real bands didn't use it."

"Good heavens above," Joe said to the room in general. "You think a symphony orchestra just gets together and wings it? The conductor just stands up and scratches the air? You pull that music out, Son, and we'll try it."

"But you just said you can't read sheet music," Skip pointed out.

"So? I'll learn. Now let's see it."

Skip pulled out a book of music and set it up on a

chair, since there was no music stand. The four men gathered around and looked it over.

"'You Are My Sunshine'?" Joe asked.

Skip made a face.

"It's cheerful," Joe said.

"I was thinking maybe we could do 'I Am a Man of Constant Sorrow,'" Skip suggested.

"Let's do 'I'll Fly Away,'" Paul said. "At least we all know the lyrics to that one."

For the next hour they studied the music, each of them trying the melody separately, then together, then with everybody singing. Paul thought they were making progress until he glanced up and saw Bo Twist standing by a pool table. The man had been eating a huge bear claw but had stopped, the pastry raised halfway to his mouth, his sugary jaw dropped open with an amazement that was not complimentary.

"Maybe we should take a break," Paul said.

"Aw, do we have to?" Skip asked. But then he looked at his watch and quickly gathered his music. "I've got to get going," he said, grabbing his banjo and case. "I'm on duty in half an hour. That was great! See you later, guys!" He ran out of the room, snapping his case shut as he went.

"Enthusiastic, ain't he?" Joe asked without showing any enthusiasm himself.

Sam nodded.

Paul looked at Joe and Sam and said, "We were awful."

Sam nodded again.

Joe sighed, but then said, "Well, let's not get discouraged.

It was our first time. We keep rehearsing, we're bound to get better."

"Maybe," Paul said. "But I keep remembering the old saying about the silk purse and the sow's ear."

KATE PARKED HER CAR in the garage and took the groceries inside, glancing at the clock as she did so. She'd have to hustle to get things ready in time for dinner. She preheated the oven and washed her hands before tackling the leeks.

While she sliced and washed the leeks, cored, seeded, and sliced the peppers, and heated up chicken broth from the freezer, she kept wondering what had happened to her scarf. Or rather, who had taken it. It certainly hadn't gotten up and left of its own accord.

She was also still upset about the scene she'd witnessed between Amanda and Renee. And while Kate put little stock in Renee's periodic tirades, she also knew they were usually based on real emotions.

But while she had seen Renee upset, defensive, and even indignant, she'd never seen Renee as angry as she'd been that afternoon. Of course, jealousy could light a fire in people and Renee was jealous of Amanda. Kate suspected that Renee was only partly upset about the incident more than fifty years ago over a boy named Charlie and was mostly upset because of Junius. Once again, Renee was sweet on somebody who was more interested in Amanda. No wonder Renee had lashed out, though that veiled accusation about nobody being above suspicion had been a bit much . . . Or had it? Kate's silk scarf was gone. And she knew Renee hadn't taken it.

Of course, Kate thought as she put the red peppers sprinkled with feta cheese into the oven, *someone else might have come into the Bixby house and taken it. But what intruder would take just a silk scarf? Why would anyone take just a silk scarf? An intruder . . .* Kate tried to remember whether she had locked the kitchen door when she had left earlier. Surely she had. But she honestly couldn't remember. Too much had happened.

Amanda had been at the house when her scarf disappeared, Kate thought, but so had Martha Sinclair, driving off as she arrived. She couldn't believe Martha would take anything that wasn't hers. But would Amanda? Kate stood looking out the kitchen window, chewing her thumb. Amanda was always so beautifully dressed, so composed, so ladylike. Surely she couldn't be a thief.

Paul's car came up the driveway. Kate collected her thoughts and sprinkled some parsley on the pork chops.

"Hi, honey!" she called out as Paul came into the kitchen.

"Hi, sweetheart! How was your day?" he asked and gave her a kiss.

"Busy," Kate said. "I ran a lot of errands. How was your day?"

"About the same. I'm really looking forward to dinner. I've been thinking about those pork chops all day."

Kate put the pork chops on a little indoor grill and popped the buns in the oven with the red peppers. The leeks were braising on top of the stove.

"Everything will be ready in about ten minutes," she said.

"Great. I'll just go freshen up."

Kate was faintly surprised. Usually Paul sat down and told her all about his day, aside from the things that, as a pastor, he had to keep strictly confidential. But maybe it was for the best. She certainly didn't want to tell him about the catfight she'd witnessed or her suspicions about Amanda Bly. Still . . . She sighed and finished setting the table.

They ate dinner that night in almost total silence, discussing only how good the food was and how beautiful the weather was. After dinner Paul helped her clean up the kitchen.

"Are you going to work in your studio tonight?" he asked.

"I don't know. I probably should," she said.

"Go ahead," Paul encouraged her. "I think I'm just going to relax and watch an old movie on TV."

"Really?" That was unusual too. Paul normally read a book for a while or caught up on correspondence until they both were ready to watch a favorite program. "Which one?" she asked.

Paul grinned sheepishly. "I don't know. I thought I'd see what was on. I'm just kind of in the mood for a movie."

"Okay," Kate said and went into her studio for a little while.

She looked over her sketches for the night-lights and for a larger piece she was thinking of doing for her son, Andrew, for his birthday. Andrew had always loved C. S. Lewis' Narnia series, so she had started a sketch of

Aslan standing on a green hill with a sunset behind him, trees clustered in the foreground. But she couldn't get into it. Amanda, Joe, Renee, Matt—all kept hold of her mind and wouldn't let go. Finally she switched off the lights and went back to the living room.

Paul was sitting on the couch watching an old black-and-white screwball comedy.

"What is it?" Kate asked.

Paul jumped. "Oh, it's *Bringing Up Baby*," he said. "Cary Grant and Katharine Hepburn."

Kate nodded. It wasn't one of her favorites, but she sat down on the love seat anyway. When the movie ended, she realized they had watched the whole thing without saying a word. Usually they had lots to talk about, whether it was the plot or the dialogue, or even the cinematography. She hoped Paul was feeling all right, that he wasn't coming down with a cold. Something wasn't right, that was for sure.

Chapter Six

The next morning Kate got up at her usual early time and put the coffee on. She'd dreamed of Renee and Amanda fighting over Matt, who'd turned out to be a toy lion who couldn't even growl. But Joe had been a real lion, prowling outside, scaring all of them, but most of all Amanda. Kate laughed at herself, trying to remember all of that crazy dream. She filled her coffee mug, padded to the living room, curled up in her rocking chair, and prayed for the blessing of God's word.

Then she opened her devotional book. The reading for the day was Proverbs 2:3–5: *"If you call out for insight and cry aloud for understanding, and if you look for it as for silver and search for it as for hidden treasure, then you will understand the fear of the Lord and find the knowledge of God."*

Kate sighed deeply and prayed for wisdom, insight, and understanding. Then she continued with her usual prayers for family and community. When she had finished her devotions, she returned to the kitchen and looked around. Two days in a row of baking and Paul might get suspicious. But that was the least of her worries. Smiling to herself, she pulled a large mixing bowl out of the cupboard. After all, she hadn't made a batch of spice cookies in a long time.

She was sifting the spices into the flour when a part of the passage she'd read came back to her: *"If you look for it as for silver and search for it as for hidden treasure . . ."* Obviously she was going to have to do some footwork to solve this mystery. Well, she'd talked to a few people, Livvy was going to do a little discreet investigating and, for good or ill, Renee was alerted. What more could she do?

There were the volunteer records. She could look and see who had volunteered when and whose meals they had delivered. Kate stirred the dark, rich smelling batter. And if she could correlate that information with Ada's check writing, she might be able to narrow things down. And there was Ada herself: One conversation certainly wasn't enough to jog the poor woman's fading memory. Kate picked up a teaspoon and began dropping spoonfuls of cookie dough onto the baking sheet. And what better excuse for a visit from the pastor's wife than to drop off a plate of homemade cookies?

KATE KNOCKED on Ada Blount's front door, but let herself in when nobody answered. Ada Blount greeted Kate cheerfully as she walked into the living room.

"Why, how nice of you to come by, Marybeth! No, you're not Marybeth. And you're not Icey." Ada looked at her earnestly and asked, "What is your name, honey?"

"Kate. Kate Hanlon. Pastor Hanlon's wife."

"Oh, that's right. I remember you now. My, but you look pretty. Just like springtime."

"Thank you." Kate was wearing taupe pants and a white shell under a gauze overshirt that was sprigged with roses. She held out the plate of cookies and took the napkin off the top. "I brought you some freshly baked spice cookies."

"*Ooh*, those smell wonderful!"

"Where would you like me to put them?"

"Right here on this table," Ada said enthusiastically. "I'll have one straight away."

"Go right ahead," Kate said, chuckling. "Would you like me to get you something to drink with those? Some milk?"

Ada shook her head, taking a big bite of a spice cookie. Crumbs tumbled down the front of her dress. "No, thank you, honey. I've got some sweet tea right here that'll go perfect."

Kate carefully suppressed a shudder at the idea of what she knew would be extremely sweet iced tea combined with spice cookies. Instead, she moved the stack of papers and magazines from a chair and sat down across from Ada.

"So how are you feeling today, Mrs. Blount?"

"Oh, I'm fine. Just fine. This warm weather does my old bones a treat." Ada held up the half cookie that was left. "These are wonderful. You must use your mother's recipe. I remember her blackberry cobbler . . ." Ada finished the cookie, then looked at her hands. "But you're not Marybeth."

"No," Kate said gently. "I'm Kate Hanlon. The pastor's wife."

"The new pastor?" Ada asked.

Kate nodded.

"It's just that you look so much like Marybeth. You won't tell Emma that I got a little confused, will you? She worries so much about me."

"No, I won't tell her," Kate assured her.

"Thank you. She fusses and frets so."

"It's just because she cares," Kate said. "I know she's very concerned about the man who came by and talked about doubling your money. I was wondering—"

"Oh, honey! I'm so excited about that!" Ada interrupted Kate, then stopped. She glanced at the plate of cookies and then back at Kate. "Do you think I could have another?"

"I brought them for you," Kate replied.

"Then I will," Ada said.

"About that man," Kate continued.

"What man?"

"The man you wrote the checks to."

"Oh, him."

"Do you remember what he looked like?"

Ada thought for a minute. "Well, he looked a lot like my cousin Forrest. No, that's the postman."

"How about his name?" Kate asked.

"Oh, that. Now it's funny you should ask, because I was reading something just this morning that reminded me . . ." Ada finished her second cookie and started rummaging around in the stack of papers on the table beside her. "But what was it? It wasn't in the newspaper."

Ada pulled out a magazine and the whole pile tilted dramatically. Kate leaped up and caught the mass of papers just in time.

"Thank you, honey, but you didn't need to," Ada said, tugging away at something else.

Kate took the armload and looked around for somewhere to put it.

"That's not it," Ada muttered. "Where on earth . . ."

Beginning to think it was hopeless, Kate set the papers down on the floor.

Suddenly Ada said, "The Bible! That's it. The reading this morning." She reached for an old worn Bible that was tucked into the side of her chair and showed it to Kate, opening it at the bookmark. "See? Here. The Gospel According to Matthew."

Matthew Lawson, Kate thought, her heart sinking. "His first name was Matthew?"

"Did I say that?" Ada asked, genuinely curious.

"No, but you did say Matthew."

"Oh yes," Ada said, cheerfully. Then she shook her head. "Or was it Matthews. Matthew or Matthews? Or John?"

"Mama!" Emma's voice carried into the living room.

"I just can't remember," Ada said. "It's gone."

"I saw a car parked outside—" Emma stopped short in the doorway. "Why, Kate! I didn't know it was yours."

"Yes," Kate said, standing up. "I brought your mother some homemade cookies."

"They're wonderful, Emma," Ada said. "She bakes just as well as her mama did."

Emma and Kate exchanged looks.

"I'm sure she does," Emma said.

Ada reached for another cookie and Emma said, "Mama, it's not that far to dinnertime. You're going to spoil your appetite."

"No, I'm not," Ada replied.

"Maybe I should put them in the kitchen," Kate suggested.

"Oh, I'll do that," Emma said hurriedly.

She whisked the plate into the kitchen and was back in under a minute, making Kate wonder if the kitchen might be as overflowing as the living room.

"I just came home to see if the mail had arrived yet." Emma walked toward the pile of envelopes lying on the floor just inside the door. She quickly flipped through them, then shook her head at Kate.

"Well, Mrs. Blount, it's been wonderful talking with you, but I need to get going now," Kate said, taking the old woman's hand.

"Thank you," Ada replied. "You come on back anytime, you hear?"

"I will."

Kate turned to Emma and said, "If you'd like, I can give you a lift back to your shop."

"That would be great," Emma said. "I'll be back in an hour or so, Mama."

Outside, Emma asked, "Well?" as they walked down the sidewalk. "Did you learn anything new?"

Kate nodded. "She said that the man's name was Matthew. Or Matthews. A Mr. Matthews maybe."

Emma gasped and stopped just as she was opening the car door. "LuAnne's husband!"

"What?" Kate exclaimed.

"LuAnne Matthews. Down at the diner. Her husband. Tom Matthews." Each brief sentence burst out of her.

"Good heavens," Kate said, stunned. She'd always assumed that LuAnne was single, but this was not the time to admit to that much ignorance. "It can't be."

"Oh yes, it can," Emma said, getting into the car.

Kate fastened her seatbelt automatically, thinking furiously. "I've never met him. I've never even *heard* of him."

"He's a truck driver. He's always gone. It's the perfect excuse."

"But in that case, how would he know your mother?"

"Tom sells natural herbal remedies on the side." Emma flushed. "N-Life. Well, you know there's not that much that can be done for Mama's condition medically. But over in Europe, they've been using herbs for decades. Ginkgo biloba, moss extract, omega-3. I mean, it's worth a try," Emma added belligerently.

Kate patted her hand and said, "Of course it is."

"Anyway, I've been buying all my vitamins and supplements from Tom for a couple of years now. You know, with my health I have to have special supplements or I wouldn't have the strength to get through the day. I put my order in with LuAnne, and she'll either hold them for me at the diner or Tom drops them off if he's in town."

Emma shook her head. "He's been at the house at least three or four times. He's seen what Mama's like." Emma's hands were balled up into fists and she beat them on her knees. "And LuAnne's got that brand new truck! It all fits!"

"Emma . . ." Kate tried to interrupt, but Emma kept going. Kate sighed and turned left onto Smith Street.

"How else could she afford it? She's a waitress! Loretta could never pay her that much. And you know what tips are like in Copper Mill. And as for Tom, well, they've always just been getting by. That's why he sells herbal supplements on the side. And what better way to find out who's not exactly . . . you know. Anyone could figure out that the people who need those herbs the most are the ones who would miss their money the least—"

"Emma," Kate interrupted, "we don't know that any of this is true."

"Mark my words," Emma said emphatically. "That truck. Mr. Matthews. It all fits together perfectly. That truck was bought and paid for with my mother's money. Now we know."

"No, we don't," Kate corrected, parking her car outside the ice-cream shop. "Emma, this is all conjecture. For one thing, you know that your mother isn't always clear about names. She's still half convinced I'm Marybeth."

Emma looked out the window but didn't say anything.

"It might be Mr. Matthews . . ." Kate said.

Emma turned back toward Kate, her mouth open, but

Kate went on, "or it might not. It might be someone whose first name is Matthew, or it might be that Ada got the wrong Gospel and it's Luke or John. We won't know until we get the copies of the checks."

"But that truck!"

"It's no crime to buy a truck." Kate stopped, suddenly remembering that Evelyn Cline had said that it hadn't been financed through the bank. "Look, you asked me to look into this. Please, let me. I was going to talk to LuAnne anyway."

"I could just ask LuAnne myself," Emma said belligerently.

"Do you really think that's a good idea?" Kate asked.

Emma sat silently for a moment, then admitted, "Probably not. I'd probably cause a scene in front of everybody."

"Which wouldn't do anyone any good," Kate said gently.

Emma nodded. "You're right. I'm too upset. I'd just . . ." She began, then went silent for a couple of minutes, her face working as she thought things through. "You're right," she finally said. "I asked you to investigate, so I should leave it up to you. And I will."

Kate patted her on the shoulder and a smile flitted across Emma's face. "Not that I don't want to go charging in myself."

"I know," Kate replied. "But please, don't."

Emma nodded again and opened the car door. Then she turned back to Kate, smiling, and said, "And at least we found out a name! Thanks, Kate."

"You're quite welcome," Kate said. "Any time."

Kate watched Emma go into her shop, then she glanced at her watch. Eleven o'clock. Maybe she could have an early lunch at the Country Diner.

She pulled up next to LuAnne's new black Chevy pickup outside the diner. The pickup *was* huge. Just getting into it must be quite a trick, and Kate was thankful that with her arthritic knee, she wasn't the one who had to climb into the cab on a daily basis. She looked at the license-plate holder for the dealer location: Lexington, Kentucky. Now why would LuAnne buy a truck all the way up in Kentucky when there were dealerships all over Tennessee? She shook her head and walked into the diner.

"Hi, Kate!" LuAnne called from behind the counter, where she was cleaning the beverage dispensers. "Be right with you!"

"No hurry," Kate replied. It was tempting to sit at a table near the window, where her back would be warmed by the sun, but she wanted to talk to LuAnne, so she perched on one of the stools at the counter and waited for LuAnne to finish her cleaning.

"Done!" LuAnne said proudly, throwing the dishrag onto a tray of dirty dishes. She looked at Kate and asked, "Leaded?"

"Definitely," Kate answered. "I was just thinking I've never seen it so quiet in here."

"Yep, we're in between rushes," LuAnne agreed, pouring Kate's coffee. "Except for those fellows," she nodded toward the back booth, where a group of farmers were talking inaudibly over their coffee. "They'll be here until the lunch crowd shows up and then they'll light out of here as fast as they can. Tell you the truth, they're only sociable with each other." She set two plastic containers of creamer down for Kate and asked, "Now, what can I get for you, darlin'?"

"Grilled cheese," Kate said.

"With bacon?"

Kate sighed. "I shouldn't. There's enough cholesterol without that."

LuAnne made a face. "Cholesterol. I don't know if I believe in any of that. Food is food, and if it's home cooked, I don't think there's anything to worry about." She twirled around to the large pass-through window, clipped the ticket to the carousel, and turned it to face Loretta, who was in the kitchen. Then she turned back to Kate and added cheerfully, "Of course, it depends some on the home it's bein' cooked in."

"True." Kate took a sip of coffee, then said, "You know, LuAnne, I've got to admit something to you. Today I was talking to Emma and she mentioned she bought herbal supplements from your husband, and I never even realized you were married!" Kate laughed. "I'm sorry, it's just that I never met him, and you—"

"I know," LuAnne said, laughing. "Tom's on the road so much, I might as well be widowed or single. I reckon half the people in town don't even know what he looks like." She caught her breath but still chuckled a bit.

"We've been married almost twenty years and I think he's spent ninety percent of that on the road. He's a truck driver, you know."

"Don't you mind him being gone so much?" Kate asked.

"Well, I did at first," LuAnne admitted. "But it's been years now. I'm used to it. And there are some advantages—"

"Order up!" Loretta called out from the kitchen and banged the bell on the windowsill.

LuAnne rolled her eyes and placed the steaming plate in front of Kate. "There you go."

"Thanks. This looks wonderful." Kate bit off a piece of crispy bacon. "*Mmm.* I don't know if I could stand having Paul gone all the time."

"And I don't know that I could stand havin' Tom underfoot all the time. I mean, I do miss him, but you can get so much more done when they're gone. Not to mention eatin' when and what you please and not havin' any fights over the remote."

Kate laughed.

"And I don't have to arm wrestle him to take me out someplace. Tom's not much for goin' out, and when he is home, we . . ." LuAnne blushed slightly. "Well, to be honest, we spend so much time apart that when he does come home, we don't go out hardly anywhere. We stay home and get caught up."

"And those herbal supplements—how does that work?" Kate asked, biting into her crispy sandwich.

"Oh, that," LuAnne reached under the counter and brought out a flyer. "I hand out the flyers for him, and folks make out their orders and give them back to me. If he can, Tom drops the orders off at people's houses, and if he can't, they can always pick up their orders here and leave the money with me."

Kate nodded, looking at the brochure. "Very enterprising."

"That's my Tom. We were poor as church mice when we first started out and I think he's been workin' two jobs ever since. He doesn't have to anymore, but he *believes* in N-Life." LuAnne tapped the flyer for emphasis.

"I'm sure they're very good," Kate said.

"Tom got hooked up with them back when they first started and now he's one of their best salesmen in these parts," LuAnne said proudly.

"That's wonderful," Kate said warmly. "By the way, I really like the new truck."

LuAnne laughed. "I'm pretty pleased with it myself. Tom bought it for me in Kentucky and had it delivered." She shook her head. "I couldn't believe it when I saw it. I got on the telephone and bawled him right out."

"Bawled him out?" Kate was surprised.

"Of course! Spendin' so much money without even asking me? I chewed him up one way and down the other." LuAnne giggled. "Then I told him what a sweetheart he was. Truth was, he'd been worried about me in my old car ever since last winter when we got all that snow and ice. Well, one day I nearly went off the road goin' up to Pine Ridge. I told Tom about it, and he decided I ought to have a four-wheel drive. 'Course, he had to get me the biggest one on the lot."

"Men and their toys?" Kate grinned.

LuAnne nodded and winked. "You got that right. I'd have preferred something a bit smaller, but I couldn't tell him that, now could I?"

Kate shook her head.

"Anyway, he spotted it up in Lexington and had his eye on it for a while, just waitin' until he got the money. So when he got a bonus, he bought it for my birthday. Now wasn't that sweet of him?"

"Yes," Kate said, looking at LuAnne's beaming face. But she couldn't help wondering what kind of bonus Tom Matthews had gotten.

Chapter Seven

Kate walked out of the diner carrying the flyer about N-Life herbal supplements. She glanced at LuAnne's black pickup and sighed, hoping that LuAnne's obvious faith in her husband was not misplaced. There wasn't any proof that Tom Matthews had done anything except get a bonus from his trucking company.

A hammering sound rang across the Town Green as Kate was about to get into her car. She looked toward the clock tower and saw a group of men busily assembling something underneath it. What on earth could they be doing? She couldn't resist walking over to see what was going on.

"Hey, Mrs. Hanlon," Clifton Beasley called out. He had moved from his usual spot on the porch of the Mercantile and was watching the activity from a safe distance under a tree.

"Hello, Clifton. What's going on?"

"Settin' up the stage for the summer concert series," he said. "Time to get her up and then she'll be all set to go."

"Are you going to do anything for the series?"

"Me? Naw. I used to sing with the Elks barbershop quartet, but my voice cracked up years ago. I just sit and listen and eat all the ice cream that's on offer." He leaned toward her and added, "And any pie that might be for sale."

Kate laughed. "I heard that this year it was going to be root-beer floats."

"Well, those are good too, but I always say pie and ice cream go real good together. Just something to keep in mind."

"I'll remember that." Kate watched as the men hammered away at the posts. Then they got some lumber and began on the stage flooring. "So who's going to be performing?" she asked.

"Well, the high-school band always plays," Clifton said, hooking his thumbs in the straps of his overalls. "And there's usually a ladies' choir. Betty Anderson started it up a while back, after the barbershop quartet gave out. Calls it the Beauty Shop Quartet, 'cause it's all women. Couple of the church choirs sing too. Every once in a while, there's a soloist. And there's usually a couple of kids with their garage bands at some point. I cut out when they play. Too loud for me."

Kate waved the flyer in her hand at a wasp that floated near them.

"I see you've got one of Tom's flyers," Clifton noted. "He tried to get me interested in that stuff, but I told him no."

"You don't believe in vitamins?" Kate asked.

"No, it wasn't that. He wanted me to invest in it. Said I had lots of free time, I could be a . . . Now what did he call it? A co . . . a codistributor. That's it." Clifton shrugged, not noticing the stricken look on Kate's face. "I turned him down. I don't need the money and I enjoy having my time to myself. That kind of thing's a young man's game anyway."

Kate pulled herself together enough to say, "Of course."

"Now, if you were to ask me to help distribute pies . . ."

Kate managed to laugh. "Clifton, you never give up, do you?"

He shrugged. "You can't blame a man for tryin'."

"No, you can't," she agreed. "Well, I've got to get going. You behave yourself, now, you hear?"

"I can't get in too much trouble with this bursitis of mine!" Clifton called back.

Kate walked back to her car, her mood seriously darkened. Tom Matthews asked Clifton to invest . . . Maybe he was just thinking in terms of having someone help him. But had Tom asked others to invest as well? Kate shook her head and started her car. It was time to go back to the Bixby house and work out that chart.

THE BIXBY HOUSE was quiet and empty. The dishes had all been done after that day's meal preparation. Kate sat down at the kitchen table and started making a chart of everyone's deliveries. It took her most of the afternoon, but by the time she was done, the chart was as complete as she could make it. Now she pretty much knew who had delivered meals to whom for the last six months. The only people who had officially delivered meals to Ada Blount, besides Emma, were Matt Lawson, Junius Lawson, and Martha Sinclair. That narrowed it down considerably. But she couldn't stop there: There were also some blank days when there wasn't anyone signed up for the duty.

She was pondering this when Renee Lambert marched in.

"Well!" Renee exclaimed. "Here you are! I've been looking for you all over. Why weren't you at home, where you're supposed to be? We've got to know where our pastor's wife is, you know." She dropped her shoulder bag on the table and Kisses wheezed up into Kate's face.

"Why, Renee?" Kate asked as kindly as she could. "Did something happen?"

"What on earth are you working on?" Renee asked, looking at the chart.

"I'm trying to figure out who's volunteered when," Kate said. "I thought if I could correlate who volunteered with when a theft occurred—"

"*Hmm*. Not a bad idea," Renee said.

"The only problem is, there are some blank spots," Kate said.

"Like where?"

Renee leaned over the table and Kate showed her.

"Oh, that's real simple," Renee said. "That's when someone didn't show up or couldn't make it. So whoever was here fixing meals made the deliveries."

Kate sighed. "So I need to add in the prep cooks."

"If you want to do it right, yes," Renee said.

Kate nodded and picked up her pencil again.

"But before you start on that, what's this I hear about LuAnne's husband stealing money from Ada Blount?"

Kate gasped. "I don't know what you're talking about, Renee."

Renee's eyes narrowed. "I was just talking to Emma about the summer concert series—"

"Are you in the Beauty Shop Quartet?" Kate jumped in, partly to shift the conversation and partly because the idea of Renee performing—undoubtedly holding Kisses in her arms—had captured her imagination.

"Of course I am!" She fluttered her fingers. "And now I'm going to be their choral director."

"Choral director?" Kate knew her eyes had flown wide open, and she blinked rapidly, hoping she wouldn't giggle. "I never realized, Renee."

"Yes, well, after all, I am practically the choir director for our church, you know."

Kate nodded. The choir met at Renee's house every Wednesday night to practice and Renee generally took charge. She wasn't sure that was exactly the same as being choir director, but she wasn't going to argue about it.

"So it was natural that Emma would ask me to direct them when she dropped out," Renee continued. "She's been their choral director for the past few years, but she said she couldn't do it this year. Well,"—Renee sat down heavily in a chair and scratched Kisses behind his ears—"naturally I had to ask why. And she said she just couldn't work with LuAnne Matthews right now."

Renee waited pointedly for some response. Kate continued to stare at her as blankly as she could.

"So I asked her why," Renee finally said, "and after a while she said she had suspicions about Tom Matthews. And money. Need I say more?"

"No," Kate replied quietly. "You don't."

"And?"

"And nothing," Kate said. "There's no proof. It's just a suspicion and I'm looking into it." She sighed and rubbed her forehead. "I can't believe that Emma is talking to people about this."

"What people?" Renee exclaimed. "She just talked to me, that's all. And I'm as discreet as they come."

Kate stifled a laugh and said, "I know you are. I'm just afraid that she might be spreading rumors around town."

"I know what you mean," Renee said. "Rumors are terrible things. And I always try to stop them in their tracks. But at the same time, you can't expect a woman to direct someone singing 'My Favorite Things' when she can't trust her."

Kate got up. "I've got to go talk to Emma. Tell her not to say anything more to anyone at all."

"Now you just settle down, Kate," Renee said. "I've already told Emma that myself."

"You have?"

"Of course I have." Renee sniffed. "LuAnne and I have had our occasional differences, but I am well aware that she would never countenance theft. If anybody's guilty, it's that shifty husband of hers. Here today, gone tomorrow. You never see him, you never hear of him, he's never there. And then there's that whole snake-oil thing."

"You mean the herbal supplements?" Kate asked.

"Exactly. If they were any good, they'd be sold in a drugstore. I remember when Tom started selling those, and LuAnne was passing out flyers to every Tom, Dick, and Harry. Next thing you know, everybody in town was buying them. Martha Sinclair was thinking of becoming a distributor herself." Renee sniffed again. "Of course, Martha would be attracted by something like that. There are some stories I could tell . . ." Renee looked down at her French-manicured fingernails. "She was caught shoplifting once, you know."

"Really?" Kate gasped. "When? How?"

"Penny candy at the Mercantile," Renee said reluctantly. "When she was five or six. But it just goes to show you that she wasn't raised right, doesn't it?"

Kate sighed. "I'm more worried about LuAnne and Tom."

"Well, don't be. Although," Renee added with a pious expression, "I always say there's no smoke without fire. But that doesn't mean that LuAnne should suffer for it. So I told Emma that her objections would be kept strictly between the two of us. Still, when she told me that you knew all about it"—Renee's look was pointed—"I couldn't believe you hadn't said anything to me."

"I only heard about it this morning," Kate said.

"Oh." Renee thought for a moment, then nodded. "Well, what can I do to help?"

"Nothing right now," Kate said. "I'm still thinking about what should be the next step. But when I figure it out, I'll let you know."

"Well, all I can say is you'd better figure out something

quick. As it is, the Beauty Shop Quartet is practically falling apart."

Kate suppressed a smile at Renee's penchant for exaggeration.

"And it's a vital part of the summer concert series."

"I'm sure it is," Kate said. "Believe me, I'm just as concerned as anyone else."

"*Mmm.*" Renee got up, gathering her shoulder bag, and stood still for a moment.

Kate wondered if she was going to say anything about her encounter yesterday with Amanda.

"Well, I've got to get going. Mama will be wondering where I am."

"Good-bye, Renee," Kate said.

Well, what had she expected, after all? An apology? An explanation? Kate sighed and looked back down at the table, covered with papers. She could only pray that Renee really had managed to stop Emma from spreading her suspicions around town. Of course, the money was only part of it. There was Betty's ring and her own scarf. Tom Matthews couldn't have stolen either of those. Nor could Matthew Lawson. And what about Martha Sinclair? She had been at the Bixby house the previous day when Kate's scarf had disappeared. But stealing penny candy when you're five is a long way from being a thief as an adult. Kate got up, gathered her papers, locked up the Bixby house, and headed home.

That night, in an attempt to break through the strange silence that seemed to hover over Paul and her lately, she asked him what he knew about Amanda Bly.

Paul glanced at her. "Not a lot. She was born and raised here, but then she went up somewhere to college, got married, and didn't come back to Copper Mill until she was widowed. Why?"

"I was just wondering," Kate said. "She's such a presence, don't you think?"

"Presence?"

"So well groomed and stylish."

"She does always look very nice," Paul agreed.

"I was just wondering who her friends were back when she was young."

"I have no idea," Paul said. "After all, it must have been over forty years ago when she left. But probably the same people she spends time with now."

"Not necessarily," Kate said. "Didn't you have some friends when you were young that you haven't stayed in touch with?" She noted a quick flicker of discomfiture cross his face.

"Sure," Paul said. "Everyone does. People change."

Kate nodded. "Like Joe Tucker. I've heard he was kind of wild when he was young."

Paul looked startled. "Yes, he was. He's told me some of it, but . . ."

Kate nodded. She understood that Paul couldn't tell her all he knew.

"But believe me, that's all in the past. Well, you know that. You know he's one of Faith Briar's most loyal parishioners. Whatever he was when he was young, whatever he did a long time ago, he's a good man now. A man of faith."

Paul's voice rang with a note of assurance that touched

Kate. She knew he was sincere and Paul was rarely wrong in discerning people's character.

"Why do you ask?" he said, his tone shifting.

"Curiosity. Truth is, I've noticed a certain amount of tension between Joe Tucker and Amanda Bly. There's some old quarrel there and I can't figure out what it could be."

"*Hmm*. I've never noticed."

Kate sighed. It was amazing how obtuse even the best of men could be. "Well, it's there. Believe me."

"Oh, I do. You can read people pretty well," Paul said.

"Thank you," Kate said, smiling. Maybe now was the time to tell him what was going on. But she just couldn't do it. Instead, she said, "Did I tell you I saw some workmen setting up the stage for the summer concert series this morning?"

Paul swallowed a huge chunk of bread whole. "No, you didn't."

"Yes. I watched for a while with Clifton Beasley."

Paul smiled weakly. "I'm sure he tried to get a pie out of you."

"Yes, he did. And I evaded him, as usual. But you know, this whole concert thing seems to be really big up here. There's one concert each week, and Clifton said everyone either plays in or attends the concerts. It sounds like a lovely way to spend a summer evening, don't you think?"

Paul's fork slipped out of his hand onto the floor. He bent over and picked it up, coming back up with a red face. "Yes, well, I'm sure it's going to be great." He smiled at Kate, who was perplexed by the strange tone in his voice. "We'll make sure to have front-row seats."

"I was wondering—" Kate began just as the telephone rang.

"I'll get it," Paul said. He jumped up and went over to answer it. "Hello? Andrew!" It was their son. "How are you? That's great! No, we've just finished dinner."

He gave Kate a questioning look and she nodded. They had pretty much finished and a call from Andrew was always a treat.

Kate smiled. "I'll get the dishes later," she said in a semiwhisper. "I'll go in the studio and work for a bit," she said, knowing this conversation would be a long one. "But I want to talk to him when you're done."

Paul nodded, and Kate went into her studio and pulled out her Aslan sketch. Andrew would love it, and it would be something he could hand down to his children and grandchildren if she could pull it off. She picked up a pencil and started to put shading in Aslan's mane.

Soon she was so caught up in her work that she was startled when Paul knocked softly at the door and said, "Kate! Your turn."

Kate went into the kitchen and took the phone. She and Andrew chatted about Rachel, his wife, and their two children, Ethan and Hannah, including all the little details of their daily lives that Kate was always hungry to hear.

"Oh, and Rachel found a really interesting Web site about stained glass that she thought you'd like. I think she e-mailed it to you. Have you gotten it yet?"

"No, I haven't," Kate said. "I'll go down to the library tomorrow and check it. Our Internet connection at home is so slow."

"You need to get a DSL line," he laughed. "Or cable. That way you can get an Internet and cable package. Then you can do everything from home and have a faster connection."

"It would be nice," Kate agreed. "Maybe someday." Having a fast Internet connection at home would certainly solve a lot of problems . . . Then Kate gasped.

"Mom? Are you okay?" Andrew asked.

"Huh? Oh, darling, I'm sorry. I suddenly thought of something and I was just . . . Well, it's going to solve a major problem for me."

"Is there another mystery brewing down there?" Andrew probed.

Kate laughed nervously.

"My mother, the detective."

"Your mother, the busy lady," Kate replied. "Now tell me more about my grandchildren."

They chatted some more until Andrew had to get going. "You take care," he laughed, "and look into getting that high-speed Internet connection, okay? You can do everything online nowadays and so much faster."

"Everything except kiss your grandchildren," Kate reminded him.

Andrew laughed. "I'll tell them to work on it."

Kate hung up the phone, excited. The Internet! She could kick herself for not having thought of it at once.

She'd never accessed her account at the Mid-Cumberland Bank online, but she could certainly try it and see if electronic copies of her checks were available. Before she'd moved to Copper Mill, she'd used the Internet constantly, even for banking.

She glanced at the clock. Nine thirty. Too late to call Emma. But the following day, after she'd done a little research, she would go down and tell Emma about the wonders of the Internet. *Who knows?* she thought, *the whole mystery might get cleared up by noon.*

Chapter Eight

Wednesday was cloudy and warm, threatening rain, which was great for the flowers and perfect for spending time in the library. Kate hadn't been able to get out early that morning, having gotten tied up with laundry and stained-glass orders, so it wasn't until almost one o'clock when she parked outside the library.

Getting out of her car, she thought once again how Copper Mill had a classic example of what a library should be: an old building of mellowed brick with green trim that would make any historian sigh with delight. Inside, the first floor was well stocked with books, magazines, and tables, while upstairs were the archives, meeting rooms, and a bank of computers equipped with high-speed Internet connections. She stopped at Livvy's office on the first floor, next to the horseshoe-shaped counter, and peeked in through the door.

"Kate!" Livvy cried, looking up from her desk. "What brings you by today?"

"Oh, a little research," Kate said.

"Anything exciting?" Livvy asked.

"I don't know yet. That depends on what I find."

"Let me know if you need any help," Livvy said, eying her friend. "Say, after you're done, you want to go for a walk? I haven't taken my lunch break yet."

"It might be raining," Kate pointed out.

"I'm not made of sugar. I won't melt."

Kate grinned. "Sure. You're on. Say about an hour or so?"

"Sounds good. It'll give me a quick break before my middle schoolers arrive."

Kate waved good-bye and went upstairs. She had brought along a notebook and pen and set them down beside a computer. The first thing to do was log on to her own bank account. Kate was a little nervous about this, because she'd never accessed her account on a public computer, but she assured herself that it would be all right as long as she saw the little lock icon on-screen. And when she was done, she'd delete the cache so that no one could follow the trail.

Within minutes she was looking at her account. She pulled up a check she'd written to Creekside Books for some children's books she'd bought to send to her grand-daughter Mia for her birthday. There was the check, with her handwriting on it. But where was the back side of the check? It was only after she'd tried repeatedly to pull it up that Kate read the small blue text that said to contact the bank if she needed further information. Well, so much for that option. They would just have to continue to wait for those copies to see who had endorsed them.

Kate logged out of the bank site and deleted the cache. Then she went back to the search engine and typed in

"Tom Matthews." Hundreds of sites came up: It always amazed her how many people had the same name. She tried N-Life and found the Web site. Then she typed in "Tom Matthews" again and he was shown as a distributor, but that was it. She tried the trucking firm and he was shown as a driver. The information was there, but it was very slim. Finally, Kate went back to the main menu and thought for a while.

She might as well try Matthew Lawson's name. One of the first sites that came up was the Mid-Cumberland Bank and Trust Web site. She clicked on it, and up came a short article welcoming Matt to the bank and giving his credentials, but no biography. She went back to the other search sites she'd been given and scrolled down the list. Most were obviously not Matt, but one of them, which only showed the name *Lawson*, was that of the *Asheville Citizen-Times* newspaper. She clicked on it and pulled up an article that took her breath away:

FRAUD AND FORGERY CHARGES DROPPED
AGAINST LOCAL INVESTMENT FIRM

The state's attorney announced today that fraud and forgery charges have been dropped against Lawson Investments after the defense negotiated payment of restitution. Jordan Harnett, granddaughter of Franklin Harnett, now deceased, had originally filed charges in which Lawson Investments was accused of filing tax returns bearing Harnett's forged signature.

The firm was also accused of making a series of transactions in which Harnett's money was washed through commodity-trading accounts and deposited into a separate bank account under Lawson Investment control. Allegedly, more than $50,000 of the funds were spent "without authority, not in the due execution of their trust and in excess of any compensation that was owed." Court documents indicated that Lawson Investments assumed the duty by written contract to support Harnett, a disabled adult, now deceased, and had been entrusted with Harnett's property. The state's attorney's office declared itself satisfied . . .

Kate read the article with increasing dismay. When she was done, she searched through the online archives of the newspaper but found only one other article about the case, which simply said that charges had been brought by Jordan Harnett on behalf of her deceased grandfather. Jordan Harnett. Now there was a woman Kate would like to speak with.

She typed Jordan Harnett into the browser and waited. A number of hits came up and she scrolled through them. As well as North Carolina, there were Jordan Harnetts in Florida, Tennessee, Washington, England, and California. She typed a new search, combining Jordan Harnett with Franklin Harnett and found the poor man's obituary. Finally she decided to return to her earlier search and go with North Carolina as Jordan's home. There were three

separate addresses and phone numbers, and Kate wrote
them all down. Then she sat and thought, biting the end of
her pen.

The fact that charges had been dropped indicated that
it might not have been all that serious. Perhaps a misun-
derstanding or an heir who had simply been mistaken
in the value of the estate. And reporters were always going
to go for the more dramatic story: fraud, embezzlement,
forgery. Then again, restitution was mentioned. She
sighed. No matter how you looked at it, it didn't sound
good.

Kate did another search for Lawson Investments and
found nothing else. But it had closed, obviously, because
Matt Lawson was here in Copper Mill.

One more search, Kate promised herself, and then she
would join Livvy for a walk. This time she searched for
investment services in Asheville, North Carolina. Thirty-
five were listed, of which about twenty were branches of
national firms. Kate doubted that any of them would have
taken over the firm's clientele, but then again . . .

In the end, she printed out the whole list. She would
take these home and call them one by one until she found
the firm that had bought out Lawson Investments or had
at least taken over Matt's clients.

The printer kicked in and once the sheets printed out,
Kate went back to the computer and cleared the cache
again. She didn't want to leave any traces of these
searches either.

"You about ready to go?"

Kate jumped and saw Livvy standing at the end of the table. "You startled me," Kate gasped.

"I can tell. Are you done? It's two thirty."

"Already?" Kate exclaimed. "That went fast." She folded up the sheets of paper, gathered her rose-colored raincoat and umbrella, and said, "I'm ready. I need a break."

Outside, the two turned right on Main Street and headed toward Copper Mill Creek. It was misting, and the grass, ferns, and leaves around them looked bright green in the warm June air.

"So, Miss Marple, what did you find out?"

Kate sighed. She'd known this question was coming. And it was a matter of public record.

"Well, I found out that there was a pending lawsuit against Lawson Investments in Asheville. An heir claiming that her grandfather had been defrauded of his money."

"*Mmm.*"

Kate glanced at Livvy. "You don't seem shocked or surprised," she said. They passed by the big clock at the corner of the Town Green and Kate waved at Abby Pippins across the park.

"Well, no, I'm not," Livvy said. "Right after they moved up here, Junius told us that Matt had been practically hounded out of his business by some crazy woman who thought she should have inherited a lot more money than she did. He made it sound like it wasn't that big a deal. Why, what did the newspaper say?"

"Well, that charges were dropped."

"See?"

"But restitution had been made," Kate said.

Livvy thought for a moment. "Yes, he said something about that too. That in the end, Matt had paid her something just to settle the matter out of court . . . Because the scandal of even going to court would have been so damaging. Junius said something about Matt worrying about his future employment prospects." Livvy shrugged. "Probably the reason so many lawsuits are settled. It's cheaper to settle them than try them, in terms of money and reputation."

Kate nodded.

"You don't look very convinced," Livvy said.

"I don't know," Kate admitted. "I don't really know Matt very well." She looked into the front window of Betty's Beauty Parlor and waved at Betty, who was working on Lucy Mae Briddle, the mayor's wife. Betty waved her scissors in return.

"Who does?" Livvy exclaimed. "I mean, he goes to everything in town, but I think that's mostly because Junius makes him go. And we all know what a social butterfly Junius is. The truth is, everyone pretty much agrees that Matt has all the personality of a mud fence."

"Livvy!"

"Well, it's true," Livvy insisted. "But to give him his due, they also say he's a whiz at finances."

They passed Copper Mill Presbyterian across the street from them. The flowers next to the front steps were soaking in the mist.

"Do you know I went to talk to him the other day and he never once looked me in the eyes?" Kate said.

"He never looks anybody in the eyes. Not even when

he's shaking hands," Livvy added. "I remember the first time I met him, I was wondering what I'd done to offend him. After a while, I realized he was the same with everyone." She looked down the street and said thoughtfully, "I'm starting to wonder if maybe it's a personality disorder of some kind. He's so different from Junius."

"Isn't that the truth."

"I'll say. Junius has just slipped right into Copper Mill, almost like he was born here. He's made friends, he's at every social function, he volunteers . . . He fits right in."

"The dancing helps," Kate said. "Any man who can dance like that is going to be popular."

"And bridge and fishing, and all sorts of stuff. But Matt . . . As far as I can tell, the man hasn't made one friend since he's been here."

"Not one?" Kate was shocked.

"Not one," Livvy replied. "It's sad, but I can certainly understand why. It's like . . . It's like he's not really there. There's something missing. How can you be friends with someone who has no conversational skills and . . . I don't know, it's like he has no emotions."

"He's got to be interested in something," Kate mused.

"Football," Livvy said dryly. "He goes to all the high-school football games and I know he watches every football game on TV. When there's more than one, he tapes one while he watches the other and then he watches the taped one later."

"Even though he knows the final score?" Kate couldn't help but giggle.

"Yes. He told Danny all about it at one of James's

games last year. I always thought Danny was one of the biggest football fanatics in the world, but Matt almost *paralyzed* him with boredom, talking football nonstop. Danny said he would have changed the subject, but he was afraid Matt would get started on finances and that would have been worse. I'm afraid Danny finally just cut and ran."

Both women laughed, but then Kate shook her head. "It's just such a shame . . . I was thinking the other day how different father and son were."

"You know," she continued as they passed a row of large old homes, "I've heard of something called Asperger's syndrome, sort of a high-functioning autism. Asperger's patients have social problems but are extremely smart. People with Asperger's can lead fairly normal lives, have jobs, the whole nine yards."

"*Hmm.*"

"Maybe that's why they moved here," Kate said. "Because, you know, the other strange thing that occurred is Matt's moving from Asheville to here."

"Before that he lived in Atlanta."

"He did?"

"Yep. Worked for some accounting firm down there for a few years after college."

"And then he moved to Asheville," Kate said thoughtfully.

"What are you thinking?"

"Well, it just occurred to me how unusual that is. Most young people move from a small town to a larger city. Not from a big city to a small town."

"You did," Livvy pointed out.

"Yes, but, that's different. Paul and I are getting older, and we're downsizing."

"You're not old yet."

"I know that. But still, it makes sense for us to come to a smaller town as we look toward retirement. But Matt's on the upswing of his career. He should be going where he can make big money."

"Well, that's certainly not Copper Mill," Livvy agreed.

"And maybe his condition is why he came here. Maybe he just couldn't handle all the people in a big city," Kate speculated.

"It's possible. He can barely handle all the people here."

The creek was in sight and they walked on a few more yards in companionable silence. Kate stood on the bank and looked down at the water coursing over the rocks. The mist made an interesting pattern on the surface of the water. It felt nice to rest.

"Well," Kate finally said, "I've told you what I've found out. Now it's your turn. What have you heard?"

"Oh, everything under the sun," Livvy said solemnly.

"But it's only been two days."

Livvy laughed at Kate's astonishment. "Okay, not that much, but some. Let's see. Mindy Corson lost a necklace and Mabel Trout is worrying about a silver creamer—"

"I heard it was both the creamer and the sugar bowl," Kate interrupted.

"The sugar bowl has been found." Livvy smiled. "It was sitting on the top shelf of the back kitchen cupboard and Mabel swears she has no idea how it got there. I figure the creamer's probably in the bathroom cabinet. Or out in the garden. Same with Mindy Corson's necklace. They're both pack rats, Kate. Mindy's the worst." Livvy sighed. "I went over to her place one time and I had to thread my way between stacks of boxes, magazines, books—you name it. It's a fire hazard, but it's her house and she won't let anyone throw anything away. Thank heavens she doesn't have pets. Mabel does."

"Cats?" Kate guessed, amused.

"Twelve and counting. Personally, I'm willing to bet that the creamer's being used as a cat dish even as we speak. The smell of her place is unbelievable. I had to go inside once and I've never forgotten it. Her daughter does go in and tries to clean up every once in a while, but twelve cats are twelve cats."

Kate nodded.

"Lawton Briddle once proposed a city ordinance limiting the number of pets a person could have and I think he was thinking of Mabel when he did, but it got shot down." Livvy shook her head. "Old Man Parsons saw it as 'an unconstitutional infringement on people's liberties,' and I'm quoting him directly. He hates cats, but he hates governmental interference even more."

"I wish I could have heard him," Kate said, laughing.

"It was pure Parsons, I can assure you. Oh, but the most interesting thing I heard a while back wasn't about things disappearing; it was about things appearing."

"What on earth do you mean?" Kate asked.

"Well, I don't know if Emma mentioned this to you, but I remember back in January, she was all aflutter because Ada was wearing a scarf Emma had never seen before."

Kate instantly thought of her missing silk scarf.

"She'd asked her mom where she'd gotten it, and Ada told her she'd always had it and that Emma had just never noticed it before. That's what bothered Emma the most, I think. That she didn't know what her mother had or didn't have. She hasn't mentioned it since, but I remembered that yesterday."

"I think I'll ask her about it," Kate said. "You never know. It might have been a present from Ada's secret investment adviser."

Livvy nodded. "Could be. I'll see if I can find out if anyone else has been wearing something new and unaccounted for."

Kate shook her head. "I don't know. It all seems so tangled up—thefts, missing stuff, appearing stuff . . . And I don't know what, if any of it, is connected."

"Isn't that always the problem?" Livvy glanced at her watch and said, "Well, I guess we'd better head back if I'm going to be ready for the after-school crowd at the library."

"By the way," Kate said as they began the long trek back down Main Street again. "What do you know about LuAnne's husband?"

"He's a nice enough guy. Don't see him much. If he gets in on a Monday night, he goes down to the diner for all-you-can-eat spaghetti. You might spot him then. Or you could always place an order for supplements with LuAnne. He might drop them off. They are pretty good."

"I heard that he was looking for investment partners once upon a time," Kate mentioned.

Livvy nodded. "Yeah, I know he talked to Danny, but

Danny's not about to get into anything involving herbs or acupuncture."

"Tom does acupuncture?" Kate exclaimed.

"No." Livvy laughed. "I'm using that as an example. It's all part of what Danny calls that 'New Age mumbo jumbo.' I was just trying to remember . . . I think somebody did go in with him for a while." Livvy shook her head. "I can't remember. I'll put it in my computer"—she tapped her head—"and get back to you."

"That was a lovely walk," Kate said as they arrived back at the library.

"I agree." Livvy sighed contentedly. "Now maybe I can have a piece of rhubarb pie for dessert tonight." She glanced at Kate and said, "I must confess that I hope there's an unlimited dessert plan in heaven."

"All flavor and no calories," Kate agreed.

"Oh. Warning. James's band practiced last night in the garage. It's even more earsplitting than I expected."

"I'll remember." Kate laughed. "See you later."

She watched Livvy walk up the steps to the front door. She was such a dear friend—caring, interesting, helpful, and always full of ideas.

Kate looked at her watch. Three fifteen. If she went back home now, she could still get some more work done in her studio. She was working on some sun-catcher orders and she could easily get the rest of the cutting done before dinner. She started walking to her car, then stopped when she heard someone calling her name. The shrill tone of voice told her it was Renee.

"Well, I was wondering where you were!" Renee said.

"I was taking a walk with Livvy Jenner," Kate said, wondering at the same time why on earth she was explaining herself. "Was there something special you needed to talk to me about, Renee?"

"I was wondering what progress you've made in the investigation. Half the women in town have lost stuff, Mabel Trout is crying her eyes out over her silver sugar bowl and creamer, and—"

"I just found out that Mrs. Trout's sugar bowl has been found," Kate interrupted.

"It has?"

Kate nodded. "In a cupboard in her house."

"Oh." Renee looked disappointed. She hitched her bag up higher on her shoulder, jolting Kisses, who gave a loud yip. "But then there's Ada's brooch and Betty's ring. What about those?"

"No word on those yet," Kate admitted.

"Well?"

"I'm working on it," Kate said.

"Not by taking a walk in the pouring rain." Renee looked up at the sky expectantly.

"You're right," Kate said meekly. "And now I really should be going home."

"Well, it's good to know that at least one of you is going to be where you should be," Renee said.

"What do you mean?" Kate turned to look at Renee.

"I mean, Kate, that I don't know what Faith Briar's going to do if there's an emergency, what with our pastor down at the Dew Drop Inn all the time."

Kate stared at Renee, speechless.

"Didn't you know?" Renee asked. "Everybody's talking about it. And I for one don't think it's an appropriate place for a minister to be lounging around all day."

With that Renee scuttled off, leaving Kate choking on the thick scent of Youth-Dew.

The Dew Drop Inn! Kate sat in her car, totally perplexed. *What can Paul be doing out at that dive? If it's true . . .* She hoped for a minute that it was all a figment of Renee's vivid imagination. But knowing Renee, Kate realized that even if Paul wasn't down there all the time, he must have been down there at least once. But what on earth for? And why hadn't he mentioned it to her? Could it have something to do with the silence between them lately?

It looked as if Paul had a secret too. And what kind of secret could it be if it had something to do with that old roadhouse? Everybody knew it was a wild place, with drinking and gambling and who knows what else going on.

Kate started the car and drove carefully down the street, turning left onto Smoky Mountain Road. She wasn't going to let this get out of hand. Her imagination was working overtime. She tried to convince herself that Paul was probably meeting somebody there, something to do with his pastoral duties. She couldn't help glancing at the church parking lot as she drove by. Millie Lovelace's car wasn't there, but then Millie only worked mornings. Paul's blue Chevy pickup, however, was sitting there.

Kate instantly decided that the time for secrets was over. She pulled into the parking lot and got out of her car. She would tell Paul all about Ada Blount, the thefts, and her speculations about Tom Matthews and Matthew Lawson. And in return, she was going to get some answers about the Dew Drop Inn so that the next time she saw Renee, she would have a courteous, definitive response.

Kate entered the church and walked into the cool dimness of the sanctuary. Behind the altar was the stained-glass window she'd made of an oak tree, representing Faith Briar's new life after the church had been rebuilt following the fire. The stained-glass glowed softly in the afternoon light. The oak pews, maple floors, and white walls gave her a sense of peace, even now when her mind was whirling. She walked back through the double doors leading into the foyer, then through the side door into the office area.

"Paul?" she called out.

Millie's typewriter was covered, her desk neat as a pin.

"Paul?" Kate went into Paul's office. He wasn't there. She looked around the office and the church, even knocked on the men's-room door. Nobody was there but her.

Kate came out of the church, thoroughly bewildered. *Where on earth can he be? Is he really at the Dew Drop Inn?* She shook her head and got back in her car. It was tempting to go down to the roadhouse to see if he was there, but she decided against it. She had never spied on her husband in her life and she wasn't going to start now. Whatever was going on, Paul would tell her sooner or later. Hopefully tonight.

She started up the car and headed home. For a moment, tears stung her eyes, but she blinked them back.

This is ridiculous, she told herself sternly. *You know Paul well enough to know there's nothing seriously wrong.* But then why was she feeling so upset? Kate shook her head as she pulled into the driveway.

Inside, she put away her raincoat and umbrella, sighing. But she wasn't going to let herself run the endless treadmill of worry. Instead, she went into the kitchen, put on the coffeepot, and looked over the information she'd brought back from the library while the coffee perked. Then she poured herself a cup and reached for the telephone.

There was no answer at the first two numbers for Jordan Harnett, but on the third, an answering machine came on. Kate waited for the beep and then said, "Hello, my name is Kate Hanlon. I'm trying to find out some information about Lawson Investments and I heard that you might be able to help me. If you could call me back, I'd greatly appreciate it." She left her number and hung up.

Well, that's all I can do for now about that. Next, she looked over the list of investment firms and was trying to think of what to say when she called, when she heard a car door close in the garage. Paul usually didn't come home until much later in the afternoon. *Something's wrong,* she thought and hurried to the front door as Paul came in. He looked worn and sad.

"Paul. What is it?" she asked, her heart pounding.

"It's Amanda Bly," he said. "She's had a heart attack."

Chapter Nine

An hour later Paul and Kate were sitting in the waiting room at the Pine Ridge Hospital, waiting for word on Amanda's condition.

"I don't see anybody from Copper Mill here but us," Kate said. "You'd think whoever brought her would have stayed."

"Junius brought her," Paul said. "He'd gone by to pick her up to take her over to the Bixby house and she wasn't feeling well. In fact, she was feeling so bad she asked him to bring her right over to the hospital. Once they admitted her, she told Junius to go back to Copper Mill and let everyone know why she wasn't going to be there to help deliver meals tomorrow."

Kate shook her head in admiration. "Now that's dedication," she said.

"Amen. She's a very special lady," Paul said. "Joe was with me and Sam in the Country Diner when Junius came in and told us. Joe turned white as a sheet. I almost thought he was going to faint." Paul looked at her with a flicker of amusement. "If there's a quarrel there, I think it's all on her side."

Kate flushed. "Well, I never said I knew what had happened between them."

"I know." Paul added quietly, "I told Joe that I'd be coming up here as soon as I found you and he told me to give her his best. I think he cares for her a great deal."

"I agree," Kate replied. "But there's something . . . I don't think she trusts him."

"*Mmm.* I wish—" Paul began but broke off as Dr. McLaughlin came walking up to them, his lab coat flapping around his lanky frame.

"Pastor Hanlon! Kate!"

"How is she?" Paul asked.

"Well, she's not doing too bad," the doctor said. "It was a mild heart attack. We've given her aspirin and done an angioplasty, and there's been a ninety percent improvement in her heart function. We've got her on appropriate medication and she's doing well. Tired but well." He smiled and added in a reassuring tone, "I think she's going to be fine."

"Oh, that's wonderful," Kate said.

"How long is she going to have to stay in the hospital?" Paul asked.

"Probably about a week. I certainly don't want to let her go home until I'm absolutely certain that everything is under control. Would you like to see her briefly?" Dr. McLaughlin asked.

Paul and Kate nodded, and made their way down the hallway to the patient rooms. Dr. McLaughlin had said

that Amanda was in the very last room. When they
entered they noticed that half the lights were off and that
Amanda's bed was flanked by machines that made various
hisses, drips, and beeps. Kate's heart cried out when she
saw Amanda. She looked so very frail, so very sick, and so
very much older. The change stunned Kate for a moment,
until she realized that Amanda's eyes were closed and her
hair had been taken out of its immaculate French knot.
The thin, white wisps of hair were unkempt and tangled
on her pillow. *I've got to remember to have someone comb
her hair before she sees a mirror*, Kate thought. It would
scare Amanda to death to see herself looking like that and
she'd probably be humiliated to boot.

Beside her, Paul bowed his head, and Kate knew that
he was praying silently for health and strength for
Amanda. She bowed her head too, and when she raised it,
she saw Amanda's blue eyes open. Amanda looked at
them and smiled wanly.

"Amanda," Kate said softly. "How are you feeling?"

"Tired," she said in a weak voice. "And a little sore.
But very, very glad to be alive."

"We're all glad too," Paul said. "Everybody's been very
concerned ever since we heard."

"Thank you." Amanda looked at Paul and smiled.

"Would you like me to pray with you?"

"Please."

Paul took one of her frail hands in his and prayed:
"Lord, you gather the lambs in your arms and carry them
in your bosom. We commend to your loving care your
child, Amanda. Relieve her pain, guard her from all

danger, restore to her your gifts of gladness and strength, and raise her up to a life of service to you. Amen."

"Amen."

"I think they're going to make us go in a moment," Paul said. "Is there anything we can bring you from home?"

Amanda thought for a moment. "Maybe a couple of things . . . Could I speak to Kate alone for a moment?"

"Of course," Paul said. "I'll see you tomorrow. God bless you."

"And you, Pastor."

Kate watched her husband walk out of the room and then pulled up a chair and sat down, making sure Amanda could see her face without straining. "What would you like me to bring you, Amanda?"

"In a minute," Amanda said. "The truth is, I wanted to talk to you for a bit."

"That's fine, if you're feeling up to it," Kate cautioned.

"Oh, I am," Amanda said, looking at the wall, "I've been lying here thinking. About my life. My husband, Walter. Renee and Charlie. I did a bad thing there. I *did* steal him away from her. It was a long time ago, and I was very young and selfish. I was thinking only of myself. I didn't care a lick about who else might be hurt. I didn't even really care about him. It was all pride. Wounded pride." Amanda's voice was thick with regret.

"We've all suffered from that at one time or another," Kate assured her.

"Maybe so. But I did wrong. I knew it was wrong at the time, even though I didn't realize until afterward that he and Renee . . . I'll have to apologize if God gives me time. If not, will you tell her how sorry I am that I hurt her?"

"Of course I will," Kate said. "But you're going to be fine. The doctor said so."

"I believe him," Amanda assured her. "But on the other hand, you never know. I was thinking of something else too. Joe. Would you please let him know . . ." Amanda took as deep of a breath as she could. "Let him know that I forgive him."

Kate waited a second, but there was no more to come. "I'll tell him."

"Good. And tell him soon, if you don't mind. He's waited a long time for it." Amanda managed a faint smile. "Too long."

"I will. I promise. You just rest and take care of your-self. I'll be back tomorrow afternoon. I'll pick up your mail for you and get anything else you'd like."

"Thank you, Kate," Amanda said. "There's no rush, but I'd like my own hand lotion and maybe a little lipstick . . . There's a spare key under the mat."

"I'll get everything for you."

Amanda closed her eyes. She looked completely exhausted.

Kate got up and walked out to where Paul was waiting, and they went home.

EARLY THE NEXT MORNING, Kate drove up Smith Street, past the lingering edges of Copper Mill, until the road was engulfed on both sides by thick forest. After a mile or two, she found the dirt road that wound up a mountain to Joe Tucker's log cabin. The road was only one lane and deeply rutted, and Kate's black Honda bucked and rattled its way up around the winding curves. By the time she pulled up behind Joe's pickup truck, Kate felt as if she'd been riding a bucking bronco.

JOE'S CABIN, small and weathered, was in the middle of a clearing in the woods, the roof sloping over a deep porch in the front. Around the door grew forsythia and lilacs, and to the side was a small vegetable garden that already boasted green onions, lettuce, and spinach, as well as the more delicate shoots of tomatoes, squash, and corn. A thin plume of gray smoke rose from the chimney. Kate walked up the steps and knocked on the door. Joe opened it, dressed in khaki pants and a white T-shirt under a flannel shirt.

"How is she?" he asked tensely.

"She's doing well," Kate replied.

Joe let out a big gust of air and nodded. "Thank God. Come on in. All this has made me forget my manners. Would you like a cup of coffee?"

"I'd love one." Kate walked in the door and was instantly in the living room. She stood still for a moment, taken aback at the floor-to-ceiling bookshelves that covered the windowless back wall. "Good heavens!" she exclaimed. There were bookshelves up to the windowsill of the side walls, and she glanced behind her to see that a narrow bookshelf ran up both sides of the doorway. "I . . . I've never seen so many books in my life!"

Joe grinned. "It's my secret vice—reading. When I was a young'un, there wasn't any money for books and not much time to read them either. But I said to myself, 'When I get old enough, I'm going to buy me every book in the library.'" He looked around with a satisfied look. "I've come close. Now sit yourself down and I'll fetch some coffee."

Kate sat down on a worn blue armchair and looked around. Books were the main decoration of the room. To the left of the front door was a minute kitchen with an old stove, a small refrigerator, and a sink all in a row, and shelving above them. On the right side of the door was a deal table with a chair placed so that Joe could drink his coffee and look out the window. Three other chairs were stacked in a corner.

Beside Kate was an old mission end table, missing a couple of slats. The armchair on the other side was a soft moss green, the seat rubbed down to a khaki color. A split-log coffee table sat in front of an overstuffed gold settee. Nothing matched, everything was old and worn, but it was all comfortable and somehow pleasing.

"Here we go," Joe said, carrying a full enamelware coffeepot in one hand and two mugs in the other. He set the mugs down, filled them with coffee, and set the coffeepot directly on the coffee table.

"Shouldn't we put something under it?" Kate asked.

"Nothing's going to hurt that table," Joe assured her. "Now, tell me all about Amanda."

Kate told him about Amanda's medical care and their

visit. "The doctor assured us that she's going to be fine. They're keeping her for a week just to be on the safe side."

Joe looked relieved.

Kate took a breath and added, "And she wanted me to tell you something specifically."

"Me?" Joe looked surprised and a little apprehensive.

"Yes. She wanted me to tell you that she forgives you." Joe blinked slowly, then more rapidly.

"She said I needed to do it right away because you'd been waiting a long time for this." Kate realized that Joe was blinking back tears, that in fact he was about to break down and cry. She put a hand on his. "Joe, what happened between you and Amanda? I know you . . . I know the two of you care about each other, but something happened to divide you. What was it?"

"It's not a pretty story," Joe said. "And it was all my fault . . ."

"Really?" Kate asked tenderly.

"Really," Joe replied sternly. "You might not believe it, but back when we were young'uns, Amanda and I dated each other. Oh, it was all on the sly. Her father was the bank vice president, and my father, well, he was an old woodsman, just like I am now. No one could say we were a good match. But we loved each other."

He looked at her from under his bushy eyebrows. "Well, there we were, young, in love, with everything going against us. And more than me being from the wrong side of the tracks. I was a hellion back in those days. I did a lot of drinking and gambling. Now I never did any of that around Amanda, of course, but her brother ... Her brother, Bob Redmond, was the meanest, most hypocritical kind of snake you can imagine. And he was bound and determined to break us up."

"What did he do?" Kate asked.

"Well"—Joe took a big slurp of coffee—"first off, he got me fired from my job. I was working down at the Depot Inn, bussing tables, trying to get enough money to go to school. Didn't start at the construction business until later. 'Course, I was so stupid, I went and got drunk afterward, and it got me in a mess of trouble that Amanda heard all about." Joe shrugged. "Young'uns. They always break out and break loose at the wrong time."

"Yes, but—"

"And then I did something worse," Joe continued. "One night I ran into Bob down at the Dew Drop Inn. Well, he was half tight when he walked in and he'd come to play poker. So I said to myself, 'Here's your opportunity to get even.' So I sat myself down at the table and, by gosh, I took every cent he had." Joe took another sip of his coffee. "Worst of it was, he had a big chunk of money with him that wasn't his. Belonged to the bank. Well, when Amanda heard about that, she broke up with me for good."

"Oh, Joe." Kate sighed.

"Yep. Not long after that, I left town and joined the army." Joe straightened up in his chair as much as he could, as if he were back in the army. "I got stationed way up in Alaska, of all places, way out where there was nothing going on and not much to do except get in trouble.

And I would have, but the chaplain there was something special." Joe stared ahead as he reminisced. "He had a way of telling you the truth that made you really see it. He made me realize that I'd been nothing but bone selfish my whole life. Even when I loved Amanda, I hadn't loved her enough to fight honorably for her. Instead, I'd just tucked my tail between my legs and did the nastiest piece of revenge I could think of. Ruined a man instead of proving myself. He showed me how I'd never be anything but self-ish until I put my life and myself completely in God's hands and let him make a man of me. And I did." Joe smiled thankfully.

"And Bob? Whatever happened to him?" Kate asked.

"I don't really know," Joe said. "I did two tours in the army, and by the time I got back to town, Amanda was married and living in Knoxville, and Bob was long gone. He left town under some sort of a cloud. One of the first things I did after I came back was take what money was left of my winnings and send them back to Bob. After that I sent Bob monthly payments until I'd paid back every cent I'd taken from him in that poker game. Took me two years on nothing but a soldier's pay, but I did it. After that, well . . ."—Joe flashed a grin—"to be honest, I didn't keep writing and stay in touch. He cashed the checks, so I fig-ured we were even. There was no way we were going to be friends."

"What a story." Kate sighed again.

"Not very edifying, most of it. But I can say that I've been clean and sober for almost fifty years now. Haven't touched a drop, haven't made a bet. All thanks to God's help. And his minister, bless him." Joe's face became wistful. "When Amanda moved back to Copper Mill, after her husband died, I'd kind of hoped that maybe—"

"You'd get back together?" Kate interrupted.

"No, no, no. I did too much harm to her and hers. No, what I'd hoped is that she'd see I've changed. And maybe we could be friends. But she made it plain that wasn't going to happen. It's okay," Joe assured Kate. "I just saw it as penance for what I did."

"But now, maybe?" Kate offered hopefully. "Since she's said that she forgives you?"

Joe sighed and shook his head. "No. I'm not going to get my hopes up. I'm just going to be thankful for what I have. Forgiveness is a blessed thing, something you can't ever be too thankful for. I know. I lived without it for a lot of years. Now, well, I'm just going to enjoy having it."

Driving back to town, Kate couldn't help but hope that he and Amanda would somehow get back together. Although she couldn't honestly see Amanda living in a two-room log cabin out in the woods. Of course, if Joe was willing to move back to town . . . She laughed at herself. *Here I am playing matchmaker with two people who are certainly old enough to take care of their own affairs.* But then Kate thought about the recent awkwardness between Paul and her. Maybe a little help was always needed. And she offered up a brief prayer not only for Joe and Amanda but for Paul and her.

Chapter Ten

Later that afternoon Paul pulled up at the Dew Drop Inn and saw Bo Twist sitting outside in an old wicker rocker, a glass of iced tea on the floor beside him.

"Gonna keep on tryin', eh?" the huge man called as Paul got out of his pick-up.

"Yep," Paul said cheerfully, setting his guitar case down on the ground. "You know what they say, 'Whatever your hand finds to do, do it with all your might.'"

Bo nodded. "That in the Bible?"

"Yes it is." Paul smiled.

"Never read it myself. Never seemed to have the time nor the inclination," he said casually. "All those big words and *thees* and *thous*. Kind of threw me off." Bo fixed his gaze up at the ceiling. "People say there's a lot of stuff in it, though."

Something in Bo's voice made Paul feel that perhaps Bo wasn't as unconcerned as he seemed.

"Maybe you should give it a try," Paul said. "I've always found it a great comfort."

Bo looked at Paul. "Now that's what pastors usually say about it."

Paul chuckled.

"All that stuff about repentance and sin . . ." Bo squinted into the sunshine. "I don't know. Seems to me sometimes that religion's nothing but a way to make you feel guilty about everything."

"That's the message a lot of people hear," Paul agreed. "But the real message is that God loves us unconditionally. We have a hard time accepting that because most of our ideas of love fall pretty short. But I think if we look around, we can find all kinds of things to be grateful for. Like right now, for the sunshine and for just being alive." Paul looked at the tree-covered hills before them, the green so fresh it seemed to be drinking in the sunlight.

Bo glanced over at him. "You preach a pretty good sermon, Pastor. Are they all that short?"

Paul chuckled. "No, but I try to keep the message clear."

"Maybe I'll come down one day and listen to one."

"You'd always be welcome," Paul said earnestly.

"I'm not so sure about that." Bo frowned. "I run a bar. What would the good folks of your church say to that?"

"I hope they'd say 'welcome.' I know I would." The two men looked in each other's eyes for a moment.

"Yeah, well, what you say and what they say might be different," Bo said. "But maybe . . ." He gestured back toward the door. "Your friends are all in there tuning up. That's why I came out here. Sounds like a bunch of cats to me."

Paul laughed and hoisted his guitar case, then went inside.

"There you are!" Joe called out.

Paul noted that he was beaming.

"Come on and get yourself tuned up and ready to go!"

Skip was fingering his banjo. "Listen to this," he said and went into a rollicking version of "Rocky Top." As he sang the chorus, Paul realized once again that Skip really did have a fine singing voice.

"That was great," Paul said when Skip finished.

"I've been practicing like crazy," Skip said. "I can hardly wait to get out in front of a real audience. Can you?"

"Frankly, yes," Paul said. "But then I don't have your voice or talent."

"Well, that means we need to practice some more," Joe said.

Sam raised his eyebrows at Paul, who nodded. "Let's try it, then. 'I'll Fly Away,' one more time."

They played the gospel song three times, bungling it each time at the transition from the verse to the chorus.

"This is hopeless," Sam grumbled. "Come on, let's concentrate."

"I am concentrating!" Skip protested.

"I know you are," Sam said. "I'm talking to myself."

"We don't sound very good, do we?" Paul asked.

"Like I said, this is hopeless," Sam repeated.

"Sure sounds like it," an old, cracked voice called out from the other side of the room.

Paul looked up. There, sitting at a table, a coffee mug in front of him, his arms folded, legs crossed, and a frown on his face was the last person, other than Kate, whom Paul wanted to know about his musical attempts: Old Man Parsons.

"I don't know as I've ever heard worse fiddle music in my life, Sam," Old Man Parsons continued. "And as for that guitar . . ."

"How about me?" Joe asked.

"You should've quit singing about forty years ago," Old Man Parsons responded.

"You're right there," Joe said cheerfully. "But all it says in the Bible is to 'make a joyful noise unto the Lord.' Doesn't say anywhere that it has to be in tune."

"Yes, but it doesn't say you should bust people's eardrums either," Parsons replied stoutly.

Joe laughed.

"Here I was hoping for a quiet cup of coffee and maybe a game of euchre."

"Later," Joe said. "We've got to practice."

"I'll say you do," the old man grumbled.

Joe pulled out a harmonica. "Let's try it one more time, guys."

The harmonica might have worked, Paul thought, if Joe had had more breath for it. As it was, it sounded as wheezy as Bo Twist. Then one of Skip's banjo strings broke with a loud snapping twang. Skip waved everyone quiet and pulled out another string from his case and began to restring his banjo. Paul ran his fingers up and down his guitar neck. He'd originally planned for the Copper Mill Players to be a surprise for Kate. Now he was so embarrassed that he hoped Kate never heard about it at all. But with Old Man Parsons in the audience, his hopes for privacy were pretty much shot. Word was going to get around town fairly quickly. He glanced over at Sam and the two exchanged a rueful look.

Paul leaned over and whispered, "So much for keeping this a secret."

Sam nodded. "Yep. I think we just made the front page of the *Chronicle*. If I'm going to be famous, I'd like to be good."

"Wouldn't we all."

"You know, I thought this was going to be a piece of cake," Sam added. "I'm starting to wonder if I was this bad thirty years ago."

"Me too," Paul agreed. "I was in a little bluegrass band with some friends in high school. I know we thought we were good, but I can't tell anymore. So much for nostalgia."

"Yep. If I'm going to recapture my youth, maybe I should just take up stock-car racing. The noise couldn't be any worse."

"No, but the damage would be."

They both chuckled.

Skip, who had finished restringing his banjo, leaned in and whispered, "Is there any way we can get Old Man Parsons out of here? He's not exactly being an encouragement."

They all looked over at Old Man Parsons, who was shaking his head. They watched Bo Twist come in and sit heavily down beside him, laughing at something Old Man Parsons said.

Sam sighed. "He's just being himself."

"I know," Skip said. "That's what I mean."

KATE, MEANWHILE, was spending her afternoon running errands, among them checking her inventory at Smith Street Gifts. They'd been stocking her stained glass pieces for months now and they proved to be popular gifts.

"We're nearly sold out of the sun catchers," Steve Smith told her, waving at the depleted display hanging on the window. "The cardinals and bluebirds went quick as a flash, and I had a couple of requests for robins. You think you could do some of those?"

"I don't see why not," Kate said. "They'd be lovely. I'll try to get some worked up in the next couple of weeks."

"We'll sell right out," Steve said. "Are you working on anything new?"

"Well, I've got a couple of ideas. I'm working on a new piece for my son, based on C. S. Lewis' Narnia Chronicles, but that's copyrighted, of course. I can do a private piece, but nothing for sale."

Steve nodded.

"But I was thinking of some small animals, perhaps, for children. Like a Noah's ark, only . . ." Kate broke off, the idea of a large Noah's ark suddenly blossoming in her mind. A large central piece with the ark and the waves, and then little sun catchers of animals accompanying it, to be hung all around the windows. That could really be delightful.

"Hot idea?" Steve asked.

Kate nodded, smiling widely. "I think I'm going to have to get sketching, Steve. And fast."

Steve laughed.

Kate turned to go and almost ran into Matt Lawson. "Oh, excuse me," she said. "Hello, Matt. How are you doing?"

"Pretty good. I just ran in to get a card for Dad's birthday. It's next week."

Kate smiled encouragingly.

Matt stumped over to the card section and then turned around and asked, "Any word about Mrs. Blount's investments?"

Kate gulped. She glanced over at Steve, but he had gone to the far side of the store, where he was restocking wrapping paper and ribbons. "No, nothing yet."

Matt nodded. "I thought about it after you left. I don't know anything about what happened, but it will be good to have it cleared up. I don't like having my name mixed up in things." There seemed to be a slight strain of anxiety in his tone, and as he glanced around the store, Kate got the distinct feeling that he was nervous. "It's not good for business," he said.

"I understand." She noted that once again Matt hadn't looked her in the eyes and she remembered her theory about Asperger's. "Did you hear that Amanda Bly is in the hospital?" she asked.

"Yes," he said. "Dad told me all about it. He took her there. Do you think I should get her a card?" he asked.

"I'm sure she'd appreciate it," Kate assured him.

Matt nodded.

As Kate started to walk away, he grabbed a card out of the rack. "Will this do?"

Kate turned back and looked at it. It was a birthday card, humorous, designed for children, and rather garish. "Well . . ." she began.

Matt's eyes flickered toward her and Kate suddenly realized that he was mutely asking for help.

"It needs to be a get-well card," she said, "and I think maybe something a little more feminine for Amanda."

"*Hmm.*" Matt quickly glanced at Kate, then at the rack, then back at her again. "Do you mean flowers?" he asked.

"Yes," Kate said. "Flowers are good."

Matt's mouth tightened as he looked some more, then he pulled out a card with lilies covered in glitter.

"And something quieter," Kate advised.

"This is hard."

"Here, let me help you look," Kate said. She looked around and found a pretty card with purple lilacs on the outside and simple get-well wishes on the inside. She handed it to Matt.

"Oh." Matt took the card and studied it closely, as if memorizing it. "Quiet?" he asked.

Kate nodded.

"Okay," he said, then looked in Kate's general direction and added, "Thank you for helping me."

"You're welcome, Matt," Kate replied, smiling. She started to leave but then had an idea. She turned back and said, "You know, Matt, I'll be going to see Amanda later tonight. If you'd like to go ahead and sign the card, I'll take it with me."

Matt shook his head. "Mom told me that I should always mail cards. She said if you don't, they'll think you're cheap," he recited.

Kate smiled. Matt seemed to memorize everything. *That must be the way he lives, by memorizing all sorts of little rules and regulations that he can live by, trying to fit in.* It was rather heartbreaking. And at the same time, Kate remembered that she'd be picking up Amanda's mail for a few days, so she'd see the card when it came. "I understand," she said, feeling guilty. "It was just a thought. Good-bye."

"Good-bye."

Kate shook her head as she walked down the street to the library. She had to find a book on Asperger's and read up on it as soon as possible. When she went inside, she saw Livvy standing at the circulation desk, glasses on, checking out books for a little boy. They waved to each other and Kate went to the computer terminals that housed the library catalog, where she found two books on autism. She wrote down their call numbers and went to the stacks. They were both on the shelf, and she began leafing through them. One was strictly about severe cases of autism, so she put that back. But the other was about the different levels of autism, the means of diagnosis, and behaviors. She took that one and went to the circulation desk to check it out.

Livvy looked at the title and smiled. "Research?"

Kate nodded. "I thought I might as well look into it," she said.

"Good idea. How's Amanda?"

"She's doing fine." Kate quickly gave Livvy the information she had.

"Well, give her my love and tell her that we're all praying for her," Livvy said, handing Kate her book and her library card.

"I will. Thanks!"

Kate put the book in her car, which was parked outside the gift shop, and then went over to the Mercantile to pick up some odds and ends. As she walked out, Emma came running up to her.

"Kate!" she cried breathlessly. "Kate!"

"Emma, what is it?"

"The checks," Emma gasped. "The copies. They're here. Inside. Come with me."

Kate followed Emma into the ice-cream shop and then to the back room, its long wall covered in pantry shelves that held all the supplies Emma needed. A large stainless-steel table stood in the center, in front of the double sinks. The right third of the storeroom was swallowed up by the walk-in freezer. In the left-hand corner was a tiny office cubicle. Emma's penchant for yellow didn't have much opportunity for expression in this rather industrial room, but she had tacked yellow fabric, tie-dyed in a glowing sunburst pattern, to the cubicle partition. Behind it was an old metal desk, covered with as much paper as Ada Blount's chairs. Kate smiled to herself. *The apple doesn't fall far from the tree.*

Emma went over to the desk and looked around. "They were here just a minute ago," she said, rummaging through the papers on her desk. "Sit down while I find them."

Kate perched on a stool and waited.

"Where on earth did I put them? Here they are!" Emma handed several sheets of paper to Kate.

Kate's hands were slightly unsteady. This was what they'd been waiting for. She looked through the copies and read, first silently, then out loud, the name, written in bold, black handwriting on the endorsement side: "John Matthews."

Kate looked up at Emma. "Well, that's certainly not what I expected."

"Maybe not, but it's obvious, isn't it? It's Tom Matthews!"

"Emma," Kate said, "it says John right there."

"So what? I'll bet that's just an alias. What if he uses an alias for all the N-Life stuff? You know, so he doesn't have to report any income to the IRS?"

Kate was amazed at Emma's imagination. "But we don't have proof of any of that. Do you have anything Tom ever signed?" she asked.

"You mean to check the handwriting?" Emma asked.

Kate nodded.

"I'm sure I do. Hold on a second."

Emma burrowed into the pile on her desk like a

groundhog, papers sliding off around her, some falling onto the floor. Kate bent down and retrieved them, setting them as far away as she could from Emma's rooting. Finally Emma rose, red-faced and triumphant, holding an invoice in her hand.

"I knew I had something!" she cried. "Here."

It was an invoice for N-Life products. Any other time, Kate would have been stunned at how many vitamins and supplements Emma bought, but at the moment she only had eyes for the signature: "LuAnne Matthews." In a very lacy, feminine script.

"Emma, this is LuAnne's signature," Kate said gently.

Emma's face fell. "Darn it. I know I've got one with Tom's signature somewhere. I'll keep looking."

"You do that," Kate said. "But I've got to get going. I need to pick up Amanda's mail." She put a hand on Emma's shoulder. "Meanwhile, I'm working on another idea. Can I have one of these?" she asked, holding up the check copies.

"Of course," Emma said.

"Thank you. Be sure to keep the rest in a safe place. I know it's hard, but just be patient. We'll get to the bottom of this yet."

Emma nodded.

"I'll see you later."

"Later, Kate."

Kate walked out of the shop, putting the precious sheet of paper—her only evidence—in her purse. Poor Emma! It was frustrating enough for Kate; she could only imagine how frustrating it was for her. Kate got in her car and drove over to Amanda's house.

Amanda lived in a little Victorian gem that was even more postcard perfect than Ada Blount's. It was painted dark gray, with white trim and dark red faux shutters around the windows. Below the windows were black window boxes that in summer were full of bright red geraniums. Instead of bridal wreath, Amanda had white hydrangeas and her minuscule white-picket fence was overgrown with honeysuckle.

Inside, the place was immaculate. The cream walls in the living room were hung with English landscape paintings and the furniture was a delicate blue. Kate picked up the mail that was lying on the blue and white doormat. There was a news magazine, an AARP bulletin, and half a dozen pieces of junk mail. She stacked them neatly on the hall table, where she would remember to pick them up when she was done.

Then she went into the kitchen, a sunny, white room with a coffee-colored tile floor and coffee-and-white-striped curtains. There were still a couple of dirty dishes in the sink from Amanda's breakfast the day before, so Kate washed and dried them. She found the cupboard where they belonged and then she tackled the refrigerator. The butter would last, but she gathered the milk and other perishables and put them in a bag from the Mercantile. She'd take them over to the Bixby house where others could use them.

The house was so quiet that she could practically hear

her heart beating. Kate took the full bag of perishables and set it by the hall table. Then she went into the bathroom, which was next to the bedroom, where she picked out the toiletries Amanda had asked for, as well as a few other items she thought Amanda might like. Kate also spotted a light bathrobe hanging from a hook behind the bathroom door and decided to take that to her as well.

Finally she went into the bedroom. The bed was still rumpled, probably from Amanda lying down before Junius arrived. She remade the bed and looked around to see if there was anything else that needed tidying. She noticed that a pair of shoes was out, so she put them back in the closet. Then she looked over at the bureau. Lying on top of it was her silk scarf.

Chapter Eleven

K ate looked at the scarf as if it were a snake. *It couldn't be* ... Then she gingerly picked it up. It certainly looked like hers. She had bought it back in San Antonio fifteen years earlier and she couldn't imagine that Amanda could have its duplicate. She looked it over carefully—the same pattern, and yes, there was that little worn spot in one corner, where she'd caught it on a nail one windy day. It *was* her scarf. So how had Amanda gotten it?

Kate glanced over the bureau to see what else was there, reached for the top drawer, and then stopped herself. Yes, Mindy Corson had lost a necklace, Betty Anderson a ring, Ada Blount a rhinestone brooch and a book of poetry, Mabel Trout, a creamer—maybe—but she didn't know what any of these items looked like and she certainly didn't have the right to start rummaging through Amanda's place like a burglar. The obvious thing to do was to take the scarf to Amanda and ask her about it.

Kate gathered up the bags and the mail from the hall table, put everything in the backseat of her Honda, and drove first to the Bixby house, where she put the perishables in the refrigerator, and then home, where she wrote a note to Paul to let him know where she was. Then she headed to Pine Ridge Road.

When she walked into Amanda's hospital room, Amanda turned her head and smiled at Kate.

"Kate. How nice to see you."

"Hello, Amanda. You look like you're feeling better." And she did look much better. There was color in Amanda's cheeks that hadn't been there the night before and her hair had been brushed away from her face.

"I am. Just tired. But I ate a nice breakfast and a lovely lunch. Now, what's in all those bags?"

"Well, I stopped by your house and got your mail and a few things I thought you might like," Kate said, setting the bags down. "Oh, and I pulled the milk and bread out of the refrigerator."

"Oh, thank you! I hadn't even thought of that."

"You've got plenty to think about with getting well. I took all the perishables over to the Bixby house. I hope you don't mind."

"Not at all," Amanda said. "Better than throwing them out."

"I brought you hand lotion," Kate said, pulling things out of the bag, "and some lipstick."

"Oh, praise be," Amanda said.

"And a bathrobe, for when they get you up and around."

"Wonderful!" Amanda exclaimed. "The trouble with

hospital gowns is that they gape in the back, if you know what I mean."

"I certainly do," Kate replied, smiling. But her heart was beating fast as she pulled out the scarf and said, "I also brought you this. It's a lovely scarf."

Amanda blushed and Kate's heart sank for a moment. "Isn't it? To tell you the truth, it was a present," she said shyly. "From a secret admirer."

"Really?"

Amanda nodded. "I think . . . To be honest, I think it was from Junius," she said almost defiantly but looked away from Kate as she spoke. "I didn't have a chance to ask him, but I found this little package outside my door yesterday when I stepped outside for a breath of air. I brought it in and opened it, and I couldn't believe it. It was so beautiful! I was going to ask him about it while we were doing the meals, but of course, by the time he showed up, I felt so bad I wasn't thinking of anything but going to the hospital. Thank God he got me here in time."

"Amen," Kate agreed. "So it was from a secret admirer?"

"Yes. I have the note in my handbag. I think it's in that closet, if you'll get it out for me."

Kate got up and opened the closet. There were Amanda's clothes and shoes and handbag. She brought the handbag over to Amanda, who opened it and looked through it. "Oh, it's not here. I'll bet it's in my bureau drawer at home. The truth is," she confided, "when Junius came and I needed to go to the hospital, he suggested I not take anything with me but my ID and my insurance card. He said I really didn't want my wallet and checkbook lying around while I was out of it. And you know, he was right. After all, you never know." She smiled faintly. "Not a Copper Mill attitude, but I lived long enough in Knoxville to be cautious, and, of course, Junius is from Asheville."

"I understand," Kate said. "I always lock up when I leave the house, but I know most people here don't."

Amanda nodded. "Old habits die hard." She had been fingering the scarf the whole time and now she looked down at it. "It is beautiful, isn't it? I've never received anything so lovely. Except, of course, from Walter. My mother would never allow it. She always said that a lady should never accept anything other than candy and flowers from a gentleman . . ." She chuckled. "People were much stricter when I was a girl. Of course, I'm an old lady now, so I suppose I can accept a silk scarf."

"I think so," Kate agreed. "And you're sure it's from Junius?"

"Well, I'm assuming it's from him," Amanda said. "I can't imagine who else could have sent it to me."

"Maybe Joe?" Kate asked.

"Oh no. Joe would never be that subtle." Amanda glanced at Kate. "Have you talked with him yet?"

"This morning," Kate said. "He told me the whole story."

Amanda nodded. "Good."

"Yes." Kate thought for a moment. Should she tell Amanda that the scarf was hers? *No, not now. Later, when*

Amanda's stronger. "Well, I'd better get going and get some dinner on for Paul."

"Thank you so much for bringing me all my things," Amanda said.

"You're quite welcome. And you let me know if there's anything else you want. I'll be up again tomorrow."

"Oh, you don't have to do that," Amanda objected.

"How else are you going to get all your get well cards?" Kate said. "Oh, and everybody sends you their love and prayers."

"Thank you. People are so wonderful, aren't they?"

"Yes, they are," Kate agreed.

Kate gave Amanda a delicate hug and left. As she walked down the hospital corridor, she thought about what Amanda had said. There was the card, but then she had only Amanda's word that it came with the scarf. What if she was lying? Kate frowned in confusion as she entered the hospital lobby. As she looked toward the entrance she saw Junius walk in, dressed in a dark blue suit that set off his shining white hair.

"Kate!" he cried cheerfully. "How is she?"

"Much better. She has some color in her face and her voice is stronger." Kate looked at him earnestly. "We all know how lucky she was that you found her."

"Yes, well, I'm just thankful it happened when it did, if it had to happen at all." Junius studied her for a moment, then he said, "You know, I've been wanting to talk to you privately. Would you mind if I bought you a cup of coffee in the cafeteria?"

Kate smiled. "I'd love it. I've been wanting to talk to you too."

"Lucky me."

Anyone expecting a full-scale cafeteria from the Pine Ridge Hospital would have been sorely disappointed. The hospital was too small. Instead, as people entered the cafeteria, they saw a refrigerated section with prepackaged sandwiches, salads, milk, and juice along one wall, a couple of vending machines with snacks and soft drinks and tall coffee urns against the other, and a steel table down the center that had two entrées in stainless-steel chafing dishes.

Kate and Junius got cups of coffee and went up to the cashier, who put down her magazine to ring up their bill. Junius paid and they went into the small dining area, which was flooded with light from two walls of windows that looked out on grassy berms. The place was almost empty, except for a nurse who was reading a book at the table nearest the door. Junius pointed to a table in the corner and said, "Let's sit over there by the windows."

"Fine." After they sat down, Kate asked, "What did you want to talk to me about?"

"Oh, ladies first," Junius said gallantly.

Kate wondered if she detected a faint note of irony.

"Well, I've already thanked you for saving Amanda's life," she said, stirring creamer into her coffee and thinking furiously. She really wanted to ask about the silk scarf, but she wasn't sure how to bring it up.

"Saved her life?" Junius seemed slightly surprised.

"Well, I suppose I did." He smiled. "Do you think it will help me in my pursuit of the fair lady?"

Kate chuckled. "Oh, it's a pursuit, is it?"

"Let's just say I'm interested. Amanda is a very charming lady. One of the most charming ladies I've met in Copper Mill. Educated, lovely, refined . . . Oh yes, I'm interested. I just haven't been sure that she's been interested back. She's a lady who hides her flowers, if you know what I mean."

"I know she's been hurt before," Kate said, taking a sip of her coffee.

"*Mmm*. I suspected as much." Junius stared thoughtfully out the window. "That's a shame. It makes it that much harder . . . Oh well, faint heart and all the rest."

"And gifts always help," Kate said.

Junius raised his eyebrows quizzically.

"The silk scarf?"

He continued looking at her—for a shade too long?

"An anonymous gift from a secret admirer? She seemed to think you gave it to her."

Junius' mouth twisted humorously. "Ah romance. Personally, I don't believe in anonymous gifts." Then he leaned over and said in a low voice, "It's all too easy for someone else to take the credit." He picked up his cup and took a sip of coffee and grimaced. "I didn't send her a scarf."

Kate was surprised. Who else could have sent it?

"I must have a rival," he continued, setting the cup down. "That's not good. On the other hand, I think it's a good sign that she thought I sent it . . ." He grinned. "I might be making more progress than I thought."

"I'm sure you're making as much progress as anyone could," Kate said.

"Well, I can hope so." He pulled a sugar packet from his pocket and poured it into the coffee, stirred, and took another sip. "That's better." He looked at Kate from over his cup and added, "I've heard that you're asking questions about my son and Lawson Investments."

Kate flushed. "I suppose he told you?"

Junius leaned across the table earnestly. "Could you please tell me what's going on? I'm worried. Matt didn't tell me much, just that you'd asked him if he'd been talking with Ada Blount about investments. He had the impression that it was somehow slightly . . . irregular."

Kate sighed, wondering how to proceed. There was the problem of violating Ada's confidence and Emma's. But she could simply tell Junius what she had told Matt. "Someone, some man, talked to Ada about investments. Promised to double her money for her. I was trying to find out who it was because, well, Ada's somewhat vulnerable."

Junius nodded. "I know. Alzheimer's is a terrible thing. My wife, God rest her soul, was developing it before she died. I suppose some people thought it was a blessing when she got influenza and died." He shook his head. "I still miss her, but in some ways I'm glad I didn't have to see her get to the stage where she didn't know any of us any longer. It was frightening enough as it was."

"How long has she been gone?" Kate asked.

"About five years," Junius said. His finger traced the rim of his cup.

"I'm so sorry to hear that."

"It took me a long time to get over it. But I don't know if you ever get over something like that."

"I'm sure you don't," Kate said. "All you can do is go on."

"And that's what I've been doing. Moving here helped," Junius said. "There were too many memories in Asheville. I'm thankful Matt got the job here too. In more ways than one." He sighed. "Would you like some more coffee?"

"Yes," Kate said. "Here, let me get them this time."

"No, no," Junius said. "One of the perks of being a gentleman is being able to buy a cup of coffee for a lady." He reached out a hand, a bittersweet smile on his face, and Kate handed him her cup.

She gazed out at the grass, the willow trees rising beyond them. She was glad that Copper Mill had given Junius a fresh start after such sorrow. And maybe Matt too.

Junius returned with fresh coffee. "Here you are," he said. "And"—he pulled two creamers out of his pocket— "I know you take these."

"How observant," Kate said, pleased.

"Well, they say it's the little things that count." He sat down and stirred sugar into his coffee.

Kate poured the creamers into her coffee and stirred. "I'm glad you enjoy living here. Does Matt?"

"Oh heavens, yes. At least as far as I know." Junius

took a deep draught of coffee and sighed. "We haven't always had a close relationship. After Muriel died, I asked him to come up to Asheville. He was living in Atlanta then. I hoped that we could rebuild our relationship. It had been rocky for a long time." He looked up at Kate, his eyes anxious. "He's always been different."

"I've noticed some things," she said carefully.

"Even as a child, he never . . . he never had any real emotional connection to me or to Muriel. No, maybe to Muriel. She loved him so much, surely he felt it. But I can't say I ever saw it. He was always . . . cold. He froze me right out. Muriel said he loved us, deep down." The sadness in his voice almost broke Kate's heart.

"I'm sure he cares," Kate said.

"I wish I could be. You don't know what it was like. Oh, we tried. We did everything we could, but it just wasn't there." He hunched over his cup for a moment before looking up.

"You know," Kate said quietly, cradling her coffee cup in her hands, "I was wondering if maybe Matt has a form of autism."

"Autism?" Junius looked at her. "Isn't that where they can't even speak?"

"Oh no, there are mild forms of it too."

"I don't know. We never heard of autism when he was a boy. I don't know what his problem is, but I do know what it's cost me. And it's a sight more than affection, though that's the hardest part, of course."

He fell silent as a group of nurse's aides surged into

the room, laughing and talking. Kate and Junius drank their coffee as the aides joked with the cashier. Luckily, they were all passing through, their drinks to go, and the dining room was soon silent again. The nurse in the corner looked at her watch, closed her book, and followed them out of the room.

Junius continued, "I don't know what it is. I just know that the one thing he loves is money. He was always good at mathematics in school. He's a whiz at finances, but by God, he doesn't understand right from wrong. If he can make money, he will, no matter what it takes." He groaned. "I can't believe I'm saying this about my own son."

Kate patted his hand. "I'm so sorry."

"Not half as sorry as I am. If you knew all the trouble we went through when he was young." Junius' mouth twisted bitterly. "Back when he was in grade school, we got called in because he'd been caught stealing money from the other children. Muriel nearly had a heart attack. She tried to make him see what he'd done wrong, but you could tell he never understood it. I gave him a good whipping, hoping that that might knock some sense into him. But in high school he got in trouble for betting on the homecoming game. When all the stuff came out around that, I found out he'd been gambling for a long time."

"Gambling?" Kate asked, surprised.

"He's an addictive gambler," Junius said flatly. "It's all part of that money thing. He gambled away almost everything he had down in Atlanta. I think . . ."—he winced, then continued—"I think there was some problem with the firm's money as well. I don't know. But by then Muriel was developing Alzheimer's and didn't understand all that was going on, thank God.

"After she died, I took him on in Asheville. I had a small investment firm that I'd built up over the years. Very small, just a few clients, people I'd worked with for years. I thought I could keep an eye on him. But . . ."—Junius looked at Kate with unmistakable pain in his eyes—"there was a . . . a discrepancy with the accounts. I managed to put it right and keep Matt out of jail."

"I'm so sorry," Kate repeated, her mind whirling. "I'd heard that something had happened."

"Yes, well, I haven't told anybody what I've just told you. Most people just know that we went under. I didn't tell them why."

"I can understand," she assured him. "You wanted to protect Matt."

"Yes. I was so happy when Matt got this job here in Copper Mill. Especially since I could come here with him. I wanted us to be a real family, a real father and son. I even thought we could maybe share an apartment." Junius shrugged and took another sip of coffee. "Oh, I know that a young man wants to live on his own, but I really didn't think I would have been in the way, and I hoped I might be able to keep him on the straight and narrow." He looked down at his coffee cup, then directly into Kate's eyes. "Do you think Matt's stolen money from Ada?"

"I . . . I don't know," she said earnestly. "I honestly don't know, Junius, but I hope not."

Junius nodded. "So do I. But if he has, is there any way . . . Is there any way we can keep it quiet? If I could convince him to pay it all back? I mean, if nothing else, I can find the money, if necessary."

"Junius—"

Junius put his hands over Kate's. "I just want you to know that I would do anything, *anything*, to help my boy."

"I'm sure you would."

"Just please remember that."

Kate nodded and set her empty cup on the table.

"Well,"—Junius sighed and withdrew his hand from hers—"I'd better go see Amanda. Please, remember what I said."

"I will," Kate promised.

She watched as Junius got up and threaded his way between the tables and out of the cafeteria.

Chapter Twelve

After a hectic weekend, the normal lot for pastoral families, Kate was looking forward to a quiet Monday morning with Paul. But he left early, saying he had to go out but giving her no idea where he was going. The nagging thought about the Dew Drop Inn stayed with her as she made herself a steaming cup of coffee, sat down in her rocking chair, and opened up the library book on autism. She'd meant to read some of it earlier, but she just hadn't had time. Now she looked up Asperger's syndrome in the index and read the characteristics carefully.

Social impairments, narrow but intense interests, and peculiarities of speech and language were the big three diagnostic factors. Kate thought of Matt's inability to look people in the eyes, and his football and financial obsessions. She read further about repetitive behaviors, rituals, logic, awkward motor skills. Well, Matt certainly was all logic and no emotion. He almost never smiled or even changed expression. And he was certainly awkward. She hadn't noticed any repetitive behaviors, but then she hadn't been around him enough to notice.

She read on about all the various forms of behavior that could be exhibited and then suddenly she sat up straight, stunned. She read the sentence again: "People with Asperger's are often considered too honest and have difficulty being deceptive, even at the expense of hurting someone's feelings."

But if that was true, then Matt couldn't be a swindler and a thief. If that was true, then how could what Junius told her about Matt be true?

Kate got up from her rocking chair and walked around the living room. Maybe Matt didn't have Asperger's. Maybe something else accounted for his strange behavior. But what? Everything in the book seemed to be the Matt she knew, even the Matt that Junius had described. Except for the lying and the gambling and the fraud. That didn't fit. Apart from Junius' words and his pain-filled voice and eyes, all Kate could think of was the poor young man who'd had such difficulty picking out an appropriate get-well card.

Kate was stumped. What she wanted, what she needed, more than anything, was to talk to Paul. She wanted his perspective and she also wanted to know what was going on with him. Kate felt wrapped in secrets, like a fly caught in a spider's web, and she had to disentangle herself from them before they became as destructive to her as they had been to Joe and Amanda.

Kate leaped up from her rocking chair, grabbed her purse, and headed out the door. She needed to find Paul. She got into her car and drove down to the church, but his car wasn't there. She circled around in the parking lot, and almost without thinking, headed down Barnhill Street, her heart pounding. She didn't know what she was going to find, but it was time for the secrets to end.

Kate's adrenaline was still pumping when she pulled up at the Dew Drop Inn. Seeing Paul's pickup parked outside sent a quick jolt of apprehension through her. *Well,* she thought as she got out of the car, *it's now or never.* She walked up the creaky steps of the roadhouse and went inside.

The stale cigarette smoke made her blink more than the dim light. The main room was empty, but she could hear sounds coming from somewhere. Coughing, she followed the sound and saw Paul, Sam, Joe, and Skip all standing in a pool of light on a small platform. They were playing something that sounded vaguely familiar. As she got closer, Skip began singing "I'll Fly Away." She stood still and listened. He had a beautiful tenor voice that made the rest of the music sound off-key and off tempo. *So this is what he's been up to,* Kate thought. She winced as the men continued to play. *It's going to be hard to be enthusiastic about this.*

"Pretty durn bad, aren't they?"

Kate almost jumped and then saw Old Man Parsons sitting at a table just to her left.

"Oh, I don't know," Kate said defensively. After all, it was her husband up there playing guitar. "Maybe with a little more practice—"

"Kate?" Paul called out, peering through the darkness at her.

"Hi, honey," she called back. "I thought I'd stop by." Her voice sounded wobbly and uncertain, even to her.

Paul set down his guitar and stepped off the stage. The other three all looked dismayed and embarrassed. As he came up to her, Kate took a deep breath and said, "Why didn't you tell me you were in a band?"

"Well, I was . . ." Paul began, then stopped. He shook his head. "The truth is, at first I just wanted to surprise you and then . . . well, you heard us." He looked at her with the same expression Andrew had once when he'd inadvertently filled the dishwasher with laundry soap and flooded the kitchen. "I was hoping we'd get better before you found out."

By now the others had gathered around.

Kate smiled and said soothingly, "Well, I'm sure with practice—"

"And we are practicing," Skip interjected. "I know we've got a lot of work to do, but I know we're going to be ready for the summer concert series."

Old Man Parsons snorted.

"Well, we will," Skip insisted.

Old Man Parsons shook his head. "Might as well call yourselves the Worst Mill Players and be done with it." He looked over at Joe and growled, "We gonna play euchre or what?"

"Sure," Joe said, glancing around at his fellow players. "I think practice is over for the day."

"No!" Skip protested as Joe walked over to the table and sat down across from Old Man Parsons.

"Let me get my guitar and we'll go," Paul told Kate.

"Guys," Skip cried, "we've got to keep practicing!"

Paul walked over to the stage while Sam put a hand on Skip's shoulder and said quietly, "It's over for today, Skip. Come on. Let's get our instruments and I'll take you back to town." Sam turned to Kate and called, "See you later, Kate."

"See you, Sam."

Sam and Skip went over to the platform where Paul was putting his guitar in its case. Kate could see Skip whispering, obviously upset. She glanced down at Joe, who was shuffling cards. He looked up at her and grinned.

"Well, it was fun while it lasted," he said. "But you caught us."

"You know secrets aren't a good thing, Joe," Kate admonished.

The grin vanished. "You're right there. But we didn't mean any harm."

"I know," Kate said.

"We just wanted to play a little music," Joe added.

"But you can't," Old Man Parsons said.

"You're a hard man," Joe replied.

"I'm telling you the truth," Old Man Parsons said. "Only one of you with any talent's the Spencer boy. Let him play and you'uns applaud."

"They also serve who only stand and wait," Joe quoted cheerfully.

Paul came up, his guitar case in hand. "I'll meet you back home, all right?" he asked Kate.

"Yes," she said. She kissed him on the cheek. "See you in a few minutes."

Kate went outside, got in her car, and let out a tremendous sigh of relief. *Thank you, Lord, that all is well. And if Paul wants to play music, that's fine. I just hope he gets better at it.* She backed around in the parking lot and headed toward home.

Paul drove into the garage right behind her and Kate went on inside. She put the coffeepot on and got out two mugs. Paul came in, set the guitar case down in the entryway, and came over to her. He put his arms around her, kissed her, and said, "I'm sorry."

"For what?" she asked, resting her head on his shoulder.

"For not telling you earlier. I can imagine what you must have gone through when you heard that I was spending time down at the Dew Drop Inn."

She chuckled. "Not exactly the best place for a pastor to be spending his spare time."

"No." He leaned back and looked into her warm brown eyes.

"It was Renee who told me," Kate said.

Paul groaned. "Renee Lambert seems to know everything that goes on in Copper Mill. How I thought I could escape detection—"

"Especially going to a roadhouse."

"Believe me, I had a few doubts about it myself. But . . . there might be a reason we went there, besides playing music." He stepped back and leaned against the counter. "I've spent some time talking to the man who owns the place, Bo Twist. I have the feeling that I'm the first person in a very long time who's spoken to him about God and God's love. Maybe it's a seed planted that someone else can harvest." He smiled ruefully. "It would be nice if something came out of it besides bad music."

Kate gave him an admiring look. She loved him so much. She especially loved the way he found God's hand working in everything. "And who says it was bad music?"

"Don't be ridiculous." Paul walked over to the window and looked outside. "It started out as sort of trying to recapture our youth, I suppose."

"Skip's trying to recapture his youth?" Kate chuckled.

"No, the rest of us. Well, Sam and me. I think Joe just likes to try anything new. It hadn't occurred to me that thirty years of not playing would catch up with me." Paul turned back toward her. "I guess I thought it was like a bicycle—you never forget. Well, music's not like that. Music is more like faith: You have to practice it."

Kate smiled.

"When you heard about me at the Dew Drop Inn, what was your reaction?"

Kate looked at him thoughtfully. "I was worried and upset. I really shouldn't have been. I *know* you, not to mention the fact that I love you, and yet . . . there it was. I had to fight against doubting someone I believe in with all my heart."

"Exactly. It happens to all of us."

"Even you?"

"Of course," Paul said sincerely. "That's why I try to be

especially understanding when people come to me with questions of doubt. After all, if a word or two of gossip can make you wonder about someone you love, the nightly news could certainly make you wonder if God really is out there. But we have to remind ourselves that He is, every day." Paul poured himself a cup of coffee. "So what made you finally come down to see what I was up to?"

Kate blushed. "Well, the truth is, you weren't the only one with a secret. I've been keeping one too. It all finally came to a head today and I knew I had to talk to you."

"Let's go sit down in the living room and you can tell me all about it," Paul said, taking her hand.

As they curled up on the couch, Kate began, "It all started with the Faith Freezer Program a little over a week ago."

Paul sat and listened with the quiet intensity that made him such an excellent pastor. Kate told him about the petty thefts, the missing money, and the swirl of suspicion that surrounded Tom Matthews, Matt Lawson, Amanda, and even Martha Sinclair. She also told him about her conversation with Junius and the statements he made about his son that didn't seem to fit what she'd read about Asperger's syndrome.

"So, you see, I don't know what to believe. Do I believe Junius or do I believe the book?" she finished.

"You're assuming, of course, that Matt really does have Asperger's syndrome," Paul said. "He might not."

"I've thought of that. Of course, I've been assuming that my theory is the correct one."

"At least you have a theory. I've never thought about it one way or the other," Paul said. "I just assumed he was your typical computer geek with poor social skills."

Kate chuckled.

"But I've got to say that the man Junius described isn't the man I know—or thought I knew," he continued. "I've never seen any hint of deception or a gambling addiction in Matt. Of course, I also can't say that I've spent much time with him since neither of them comes to Faith Briar. He's . . . It's like he's always in the background. You don't really notice him."

"That's how I've felt," Kate agreed. "And that's almost exactly what Livvy said."

"Well, at least it's not just me," Paul said, almost with relief. Then he shook his head. "I should have tried harder. I've let him stay in the background instead of making an effort to draw him out."

Kate nodded, thinking that she had been guilty of the same thing.

"The Faith Freezer Program trouble worries me," Paul said, looking at Kate. "This is a serious situation. I wonder if any other elderly people have been bilked of their money?"

Kate sighed. "I've wondered the same thing. But it's not exactly something you can go around asking people about without causing the very panic I've been trying to avoid."

"True. And you say Emma believes that LuAnne's husband is involved?"

"Fixated, I think would be the best term."

Paul winced. "That's bad. I only met Tom Matthews once, at the diner. Seems nice enough. But seeming isn't being."

"I can't believe you never told me LuAnne was married," Kate said, pouting a little.

"I'm sorry. From now on, I'll tell you every time I find out someone is married," Paul said, smiling.

He paused, then admitted, "This is a hard one to figure out."

"Tell me about it. If Jordan Harnett would only call me back, I might be able to cross Matt off my list."

"Who?"

Kate told Paul about the newspaper article she'd found online. "I've left messages on her answering machine, but that's all I can do."

Paul took her hand in his and held it as they sat in silence for a moment, a happy, companionable silence, and then Kate asked, "What do you think about the scarf?"

"I don't know," he confessed. "I'm inclined to believe that Amanda received it as a present, but that means someone stole it."

"I know," Kate agreed.

"The question is, who?"

"Junius assured me that he didn't give it to her. And she says she knows it wasn't Joe. But I can't think of anyone else who would have given it to her."

Paul sighed. "Unfortunately, no matter which way you look at it, somebody has committed a crime. But we have to be very careful about accusations. And I know you have been," he added as Kate started to protest. "But even speculation has its dangers. It's all too easy to let our personal feelings about someone influence our suspicions."

"Like with Matt," Kate offered.

Paul nodded.

Or Renee, Kate could have said. She didn't tell Paul about her fleeting thought that Renee might have stolen the scarf and sent it to Amanda to set her up. Kate thought about it again now, carefully, and dismissed it. Renee was a busybody and a gossip, but she was no thief. But Kate knew it had been her own difficult relationship with Renee that had made the thought even possible.

What had Amanda said about the card that came with the scarf? Amanda was going to show it to her, but it wasn't in her purse at the hospital. It was in Amanda's bureau drawer at her home. All Kate had to do the next time she went over was to take a peek at it. She could make sure it existed and she could see the handwriting . . .

"Kate?"

She jumped and shifted her attention back to Paul.

Paul was looking at her closely. "Where did you drift off to?"

"Oh, I was thinking of how people don't write much any more. Not like in the old days. I'll bet Amanda still has all the letters Joe ever wrote to her and vice versa." She smiled at Paul, then breathed a sigh of relief when the telephone rang.

"But we do have new ways to communicate," Paul said as he went to the kitchen to answer it.

"Bobby," he said, laughing.

It was Bobby Evans, pastor of First Baptist, and Kate knew that conversation would take a while. Those two could talk for hours about the most arcane things. Kate decided to go to her studio and get some work done on her sun catchers.

Much later, Kate straightened up from her cutting table and stretched. Her back was aching from leaning over for so long cutting glass. She had two more Band-Aids on her fingers than she'd started with earlier in the day, from nicking herself on sharp edges. It was an occupational hazard of working with glass.

She stretched again, moving slowly in all directions, then she walked over to her drawing table and looked down at the Narnia sketch. It was almost done. The Noah's ark idea came back to her, so she sat down and drew a large oval with a boat in the center. But the boat wasn't quite right. *I'll have to do some research on that.* Just for fun, she doodled a couple of animals that she thought children might like: a camel, then a zebra. Then she drew an armadillo. *You can take the girl out of Texas, but you can't take the Texas out of the girl,* she thought, laughing. She didn't know how popular that one would be, but she liked it. *Maybe I'll make a couple for Ethan and Hannah,* she thought. *Remind them they've got a Texan grandmother.*

Kate yawned. She set aside her sketches, got up, and left the studio, turning out the lights behind her. As she passed Paul's study, she could hear him rustling papers.

She wandered into the living room, sat down on the couch, and picked up the remote. Beside it, on the coffee table, was the book on autism she'd checked out of the library. What if Matt wasn't autistic? What if Junius was right not to believe it? What if he'd been telling her the truth? Kate pursed her lips. *But what if I'm right?* What if Matt did have Asperger's and Junius was lying? And if Junius was lying about Matt, he could easily have been lying about the scarf and . . .

Kate leaped up and went back to her studio, where she'd put the Faith Freezer Program schedule she'd worked out. She pulled out the schedule from her file cabinet and looked at it carefully. She remembered Renee telling her that the blank days, the days when nobody was scheduled to deliver meals to Ada Blount, were days when the prep staff made the deliveries themselves. She looked at the blanks and noticed that each time Junius had delivered the meals the day before. And afterward, it was often a week before Junius was scheduled again. That might not mean anything, but then again . . .

Kate looked at the clock. A quarter to ten. She wished she could call Livvy just to talk, but she didn't dare. One thing Kate had learned the hard way was that people in a small town went to bed much earlier than people in a big city. Most people in Copper Mill were sound asleep by ten o'clock and many were up by five. She'd have to wait. Kate folded up the schedule and put it in her purse.

Chapter Thirteen

The next day, Kate went over to Amanda's to pick up her mail. She let herself in and picked up the cards that had fallen on the doormat, set them on the hall table, and then went into Amanda's bedroom. She opened the bureau drawer and found Amanda's wallet and checkbook, just as Amanda had said, sitting on top of some neatly folded handkerchiefs and gloves. But that was all. There was no card.

Kate stood there wondering whether there had ever been a card. Was Amanda the thief? Not of Ada's money, of course, but of all the knickknacks and jewelry that had disappeared? Or had Junius lied and pocketed the note so that no one would ever know that he had stolen Kate's scarf and given it to Amanda? There was no way of knowing. For a moment Kate was tempted to search for Betty's ring and that rhinestone brooch she'd heard about, but she stopped herself. She remembered Paul's warning against making accusations. It wouldn't be right and she would never be able to look Amanda in the face again if she did that.

Kate shook her head, then picked up the mail in the entry way and left. Paul was going to see Amanda that night, so he could take the cards to her.

THE FOLLOWING DAY it rained, and Kate stayed home working on her stained glass all day, but Thursday morning was so beautiful that she just had to get out. She picked up Amanda's mail—again resisting the temptation to search for jewelry—and headed over to the Country Diner to meet Paul for lunch. The sunlight was so dazzling that the diner seemed especially dark when she went inside and it took her a moment to realize that she was alone. Not only were there no customers, LuAnne wasn't there either.

Puzzled, Kate went over to the kitchen pass-through window and called out, "LuAnne? Loretta?"

"She'll be back in a minute," Loretta said, her head bobbing up in the window.

"I was just checking to make sure you hadn't closed for some reason."

"Not hardly," Loretta said, her head disappearing. Then it bobbed back up again and she said, "I made cinnamon rolls."

"Thanks," Kate said.

She sat down on a stool to wait, when LuAnne came in from the back. "Hi, LuAnne!" she said and then stopped. LuAnne's eyes were red, as if she'd been crying. "LuAnne, what's wrong?"

LuAnne bit her lip and then started crying. Kate got up off the stool, her purse and Amanda's mail falling onto the floor as she put her arms around her friend. The two

held each other for a few minutes—Kate was grateful that
no one else came into the diner just then—and then
LuAnne pulled back and wiped her eyes. She looked
around for a handkerchief and Kate handed her some
napkins.

"Here, LuAnne," she said. "What's wrong? Is it . . .
Nothing's happened to Tom, has it?"

LuAnne blew her nose loudly, shaking her head.
"No . . ."

Kate waited while LuAnne pulled herself together
enough to be able to talk.

"I'm sorry," LuAnne finally said.

"It's okay."

"It's just that . . ." LuAnne looked around the diner
helplessly. "It's just I can't believe what's going on."

"What is it?" Kate asked.

"It's Tom," LuAnne said. "Everybody's talkin' . . . and
he's not a thief!"

Kate was aghast. Obviously word had gotten out about
Emma's suspicions. "Of course he's not," she said as
soothingly as she could.

"And now I've been told that I'm not welcome in the
Beauty Shop Quartet." LuAnne blew her nose again.

"Who said that?" Kate asked.

"Renee," LuAnne replied. Her chin was trembling,
but Kate felt sure that now it was more from anger than
grief. "How dare she accuse Tom of anything! He's never
broken the law in his life! And just because he's always on
the road . . ."

"I know," Kate said.

"You've heard too?" LuAnne asked.

Kate nodded.

LuAnne's tears had dried up and a red flush now covered her face. "Gossip is just like wildfire in this town. And the worst bunch of gossipers is that group down at the beauty shop! How on earth can anybody believe such a thing? And there he is, over in North Carolina on his way down to Florida, and I'm here . . . Kate, you've got to help me. There's got to be a way we can clear his name."

Kate rested her hand on LuAnne's arm and said, "There is. I've been looking into things—"

"You have?" LuAnne asked plaintively.

Kate nodded. "Yes, I have. And I can tell you right now, the thing that would help clear up everything would be a sample of Tom's handwriting. His signature. Do you have one handy?"

LuAnne nodded. "Of course I do. Not here. But I've got piles of checks and everything at home. In fact, I'll run right home and get it for you. Loretta!"

Loretta stuck her head out the kitchen window. "You go run along, LuAnne. Do what you need to do. I'll tell folks to help themselves to coffee."

"Back in a minute," LuAnne said and hurried out the front door straight into Renee Lambert. Kate could tell LuAnne was choking back tears as she ran to her truck.

"Well, I never . . . What in the world is the matter with her?" Renee asked. "And where on earth is she going?"

Kate couldn't remember the last time she had been so angry. "Renee, did you tell LuAnne that she had to drop out of the Beauty Shop Quartet?"

Renee hitched her bag higher on her shoulder, bouncing Kisses, who sneezed. "I most certainly did not," she stated. "I simply suggested that she consider it."

"Renee!" Kate was almost ready to cry herself. "How could you?"

"How could I what? I'm not the one who's done anything wrong! I simply let LuAnne know what was being said so that she could prepare herself. I didn't say a word to anyone else. But I felt that it was my Christian duty to talk to LuAnne."

Kate groaned.

"If Tom was arrested and LuAnne didn't know a thing about it beforehand, it would likely kill the poor woman."

"But Tom isn't going to be arrested," Kate said.

"Are you sure?" Renee said with intense interest. "What have you found out?"

Kate rolled her eyes and bent over to pick up her purse and Amanda's mail. When she rose back up, Renee was standing right next to her. "Well?"

"Well, Renee," Kate said, "I'm waiting on some long-distance phone calls that might clear up the whole thing."

Kate had called the three numbers for Jordan Harnett every day, each time leaving a message on the one with the answering machine and she was hoping, no praying, that at some point she'd get a response.

"Tom's employer?" Renee asked.

"No," Kate said shortly.

"Now, Kate," Renee said, sitting down on a stool and putting her shoulder bag on the counter, "you know you can tell me."

Instead of answering, Kate asked, "Did you know Amanda's coming home tomorrow?"

"Is she well enough?" Renee asked.

"The doctors think so," Kate replied. "I've been up to see her almost every day."

"Well, that's sweet of you," Renee said. "I went up myself yesterday."

"You did?" Kate tried to hide her surprise.

"Yes, with Betty Anderson." Renee toyed with Kisses' ears. "Amanda showed us a scarf she got. From a secret admirer."

"Yes, I know," Kate said.

"She thinks Junius gave it to her!" Renee hissed, her face flushed. Her voice rose steadily as she said, "I don't believe that for a minute. And why wouldn't he just come right out and say it if he had, instead of all that nonsense?"

"That's what Junius—" Kate tried to interrupt, but Renee went on like a steamroller.

"The only reason she thinks anything of the kind is because she's the type who thinks every man is dangling after her! Always has been. A man's polite and she thinks he's in love with her. Junius, indeed. I don't know where that scarf came from, but I'm sure he would never make such a juvenile gesture."

Kate finally got up the voice to interrupt. "Renee, listen to me."

Renee became still and silent, blinking rapidly as she looked at Kate.

"I have a secret to tell you."

That got Renee's full attention, as Kate knew it would.

"There's a problem with the scarf." Kate leaned over and whispered, "It's really mine. It was stolen."

"No!" Renee gasped. "Stolen?"

"*Shh.*" Kate put a finger to her lips. "It was taken from the Bixby house. I'm keeping it a secret until I can find out who sent it to Amanda."

Renee digested that tidbit for a moment, then said, as Kate had expected, "Maybe Amanda stole it and claimed someone sent it to her."

"I don't think so," Kate said. "She seemed genuinely surprised."

Renee gazed at the coffee urn behind the counter, an odd look in her eyes.

"Renee, have you received any presents from a secret admirer? Or from a not-so-secret admirer? Like Junius?"

Renee's eyes flickered back to Kate and she stammered, "N-n-no. Of course not. He and I are just . . . we're just friends."

"I was just wondering," Kate said, fairly certain that Renee wasn't telling the exact truth. "Because it seemed to me that the two of you were getting along pretty well at the dance a couple of weeks ago."

Renee looked around uncomfortably and fluttered her fingers. "I-I just remembered I have an appointment," she stammered again, then leaped to her feet, knocking Amanda's cards onto the floor, and almost ran out of the diner.

"Well, whatever you said certainly got her up and out of here in a hurry," Loretta called from the kitchen window.

"I think I may have asked her a question she didn't like." Kate chuckled and bent down to pick up the cards again.

"There's a lot of those," Loretta said grimly. "Renee likes to ask the questions, not answer them. You want to order something?"

"I'll wait till LuAnne gets back."

"Suit yourself. You missed one under the table, behind you."

Kate picked up the card and stuffed it with the rest in her bulging purse as LuAnne came back in.

"I remembered when I got about halfway home," LuAnne said, out of breath. "The truck registration!"

She handed the document to Kate, who looked at the signature. "Tom Matthews" was written in a masculine handwriting that slanted to the left. Kate remembered the copy of the check that was back in the folder in her studio.

"Well?" LuAnne asked.

"Honestly, LuAnne, I need something I can take with me. I don't have the check—" Kate stopped, remembering that Emma had the rest at her shop. "Can I borrow your telephone to call Emma?"

"Emma's gone to Pine Ridge," LuAnne said, flushing so much that Kate didn't dare ask how she knew.

"Okay," Kate said. "Listen, I'm going to run home and get something to compare this to. If Paul comes in, would you tell him I'll be right back?"

"I sure will."

"I'll be back as quick as I can."

THE COPPER MILL PLAYERS had continued to practice in the mornings, but Paul's heart wasn't really in it anymore. Nor was Sam's.

"I'd rather be fishing," Paul whispered to Sam as he packed up his guitar.

"So would I," Sam agreed. "Listen, I've gotten some new lures in. Come on by the Mercantile and I'll show them to you."

"Sounds good," Paul replied. "I'm meeting Kate down at the diner for lunch, so I'll swing by on my way."

Sam nodded and headed out, taking Skip with him. Paul was walking off the stage when Joe, who'd ridden out with him that day, came up to him with Bo Twist by his side. "Hey, Paul. You got a minute?"

"Sure," Paul said.

"Bo's truck broke down and he needs a couple of things from the store. Would you mind giving him a ride into town, as well as me? I can give him a ride back. My truck's supposed to be out of the shop this afternoon."

"Sorry to cause you trouble," Bo apologized. "It's just I've got to stop by the pharmacy and pick up a prescription. You can just drop me off there."

"No problem," Paul said.

The three walked outside and Paul drifted back a bit, pulling Joe aside. "Is there room for the three of us?" he asked in a low voice.

Joe chuckled. "I'll ride in the back," he replied.

He climbed in the back of Paul's pickup truck, saying, "I can take the air!"

"It's the jolts I'd worry about," Paul called up to him.

"I can use my stick as a brace!" Joe said.

Paul got in the cab. When Bo climbed in beside him,

the truck sagged to the right. Paul put the truck in gear and it bounced over the railroad tracks as he pulled onto Barnhill Street.

"Thanks so much," Bo said, wiping a bead of sweat off his forehead with a handkerchief. "I need my asthma medication. I'm a martyr to my allergies."

"Sorry to hear that."

"Yeah, well, I could move to the southwest where the air is clear, but then I'd miss all this." Bo waved his hand at the mountain landscape all around them. "I couldn't stand a desert."

Paul smiled. "You've lived here all your life?"

"Most of it. There was a time . . . Well, my mother ran off from my daddy and took me with her."

"I'm sorry." Paul watched Bo out of the corner of his eye as the truck turned right onto Smith Street.

Bo shrugged. "I couldn't blame her. My daddy was a hard-drinkin' man and he was somethin' fierce. Scary. That's why Mama ran off. He owned the Dew Drop Inn, you know, and a roadhouse isn't the best thing for a drinkin' man to own. That's one thing I didn't inherit from him, praise be." Bo sighed as Paul turned left onto Ashland. "Mama and I, we moved down to Mississippi. Hated it. Hot, humid . . . But don't get me wrong; it wasn't a bad life. When I was twelve, Mama married Vern Twist, and he adopted me. Then when my daddy died, I inherited the roadhouse. I'll tell you what, I couldn't wait to get back up here to God's country. Been here ever since. Thirty years this summer."

"That's quite a story," Paul said, stopping outside the pharmacy across from Willy's Bait and Tackle.

Bo got out of the truck with a series of heaves and grunts, then he waved as he walked inside. A few minutes later, he came back out, huffing and puffing, and climbed back inside the truck. Paul made a U-turn and drove back to Smith Street, then parked in front of the Mercantile. He went around the back of the truck to help Joe get down from the flatbed.

"You blown away yet?" Paul asked.

"Nah," Joe said. "I'm just fine."

The three went into the Mercantile. Sam and Skip had already arrived, and Sam was helping Arlene Jacobs, one of his part-time checkers, redecorate the camping equipment display. Skip, who was obviously not in a hurry to get to his shift, was looking at a duck call. As Joe and Paul came up, Skip put the duck call to his lips and blew in it. The loud, flat quack made them all jump.

"Kind of a merganser sound, don't you think?" Skip commented.

"What do you know about mergansers?" Joe asked.

"Just that there are some," Skip admitted. He blew the device again and said, "I think it sounds kind of like a kazoo."

"No, it doesn't," Sam said, shaking his head.

"Well, of course, not exactly," Skip snapped. "You can only get one sound out of this. A kazoo's different. You got any here?" he asked Sam.

"Over in the toy section."

Skip was back in a minute with a blue kazoo. He put it to his lips and blew a loud, flat quack. Everyone chuckled and he turned it into a quacking march that sounded vaguely familiar.

"'Stars and Stripes Forever!'" Paul called.

Skip grinned.

"I want to try that," Joe said. He ran over to the toy rack and got three more kazoos. He handed one to Paul, who took it and blew into it experimentally, and one to Sam, who shook his head.

"I'm not playing a kazoo," Sam said.

"Ah, don't be such a stuffed shirt," Joe said, quacking at him. "Live a little!"

"Don't blow," Skip said to Paul. "You hum into them."

"That's right," Paul said. "I always forget." He tried again and did better.

"I can't sell these after y'all have had your mouths all over them, you know!" Sam snapped.

Joe reached in his wallet and pulled out a twenty-dollar bill, which he slapped down on the counter. "Now play!"

Sam glared, but as the other three started playing the Sousa march, he caught their enthusiasm and joined in. Next they kazooed the famous "Marines' Hymn," humming the well-known lyrics "From the halls of Montezuma to the shores of Tripoli," and by the time they started in on a kazoo version of "Anchors Aweigh," all of the customers, including Bo Twist, were gathered around, listening and laughing. When they stopped, it was only because the players themselves were all laughing too hard to continue.

"That's about the most fun I've had in ages," Joe said, trying to catch his breath. He looked out at the small crowd that had gathered and asked, "Y'all enjoy that?"

"Yes!" the audience cheered. "You bet!"

"Mama, mama!" cried a young boy. "Can I have one of them things?"

"I don't know . . ." his mother said.

"Oh, please. Please?" he begged. "Please?"

"Oh, I suppose." She finally gave in. "What your father will think, I don't know. And you're not to play it in the house!" she called after him as he raced to the toy section.

"You know what we ought to do?" Paul turned to his fellow players.

"What?" Sam asked.

"We ought to take these up to the hospital and play for the patients. Might cheer them up."

"Or kill them," Sam said.

Skip, who was still playing his kazoo, nodded and segued into "I'll Fly Away."

"And the hospital might object," Sam pointed out.

"That's true," Joe said. "But I think I got a better idea."

"What?" Sam asked, cautiously.

"I'll tell you tomorrow when we practice." Joe whispered in Paul's ear.

Paul nodded, the smile on his face getting wider and wider all the time.

"See?" Joe pointed to Paul. "He agrees with me."

"I don't like the sound of this," Skip said.

"I might have to charge you extra if you'uns is gonna

play them things early in the morning," Bo said, wiping his eyes.

"Then we'll charge you back for the workout we just gave you," Joe rallied.

"You got me there," Bo replied. "Think your truck's ready yet?"

"They said twelve." Joe checked his watch. "It's twelve thirty now."

Paul gasped. "Oh no! I'm supposed meet Kate for lunch." He hurriedly said good-bye to the others, then dashed across the street. He slid into the diner and looked around for Kate. She wasn't there.

"LuAnne," he said, "Have you seen Kate?"

"Not for a while," LuAnne replied, looking, Paul thought, surprisingly worried. "She ran home, saying she'd be just a minute, and she hasn't gotten back yet. But she said to tell you she'd be back here for lunch."

"Okay," Paul said. "I'll just wait."

KATE DROVE HOME from the diner in a flurry of excitement. At last, one mystery would be solved! She just hoped it wasn't Tom Matthews' handwriting on those checks. LuAnne would be devastated. She was practically a wreck as it was and who could blame her? Kate pulled into the garage, and as she was walking to the door, she heard the telephone ringing. She unlocked the door as quickly as she could and ran to the kitchen, hoping that whoever it was would be worth the hurry, and not just another telemarketer.

She pounced on the telephone, dropping her purse on the counter, where it promptly popped open, spilling its contents everywhere. "Hello?"

"Hello," a woman replied. "Is this Kate Hanlon?"

"Yes, it is."

"I'm Jordan Harnett."

Kate sat down in a kitchen chair, her heart pounding. "Oh, thank goodness. I've been trying to reach you for days."

"So I gathered from my answering machine. I've been out of town. You wanted to ask me about Lawson Investments? Do you have money with them?"

"No," Kate said. "But I'm worried about someone else. An elderly lady. I read the article about the settlement on the *Asheville Citizen-Times* Web site, and I hoped you wouldn't mind answering some questions."

"You want to know what happened," Jordan said flatly. "Well, it's quite simple, really. My grandfather was in a nursing home. He'd invested his money with Junius Lawson and—"

"Excuse me," Kate interrupted. "Did you say Junius Lawson? What about his son, Matt?"

"Oh, he came into the firm later. No, Junius was the man my grandfather knew at the beginning."

"So Junius was handling your father's estate."

"Well . . ." Jordan's voice was hesitant. "At the end, I can't really say. You see, I didn't find out what was going on until after my grandfather died. When the will was probated, I contacted the investment firm and found out that all the money was gone. Well, that didn't sound right to me, so I asked for an accounting and that was mighty hard to get, let me tell you. They basically gave me the runaround, until I told them I'd have the law on them if they didn't give me the paperwork."

"And did they?"

"Yes, but it still seemed fishy. I took it to another accountant to look over and he said it wasn't right. There were a series of commodity trading accounts, whatever those are, that ended up in some kind of estate fund that Lawson Investments controlled. I didn't understand half of what he said, to be honest. I just knew that the firm stole my grandfather's money. So I asked for the money back and when they declined, I filed suit."

"But it didn't go to trial," Kate said.

"No, they settled it out of court. I mean, there was enough scandal going on without that. I'm sure their clients were leaving in droves. As it was, they eventually closed down. Are they back in operation?"

"No," Kate said. "But there is a question of private investing."

"Oh no."

Kate could hear Jordan sigh over the telephone.

"I honestly don't know what to say. Be careful. I never trusted Junius Lawson; he was a little too smooth for me. But then it was Matt Lawson who offered the settlement and signed the check. I don't know who he was trying to protect, his father or himself or both, and frankly, I didn't care as long as the check was good. I just took the money. I figured I was lucky to get it and it saved on court costs."

"I see."

"Sorry I can't help you more."

"No, you've been a great help," Kate assured her. "Thank you for calling me back."

"No problem. Let me know if there's any other information I can give you."

"Oh," Kate said, "I do have one other question. Those trading accounts—were any of them under the name John Matthews?"

There was silence, then Jordan said, "It does sound familiar. Maybe the name of a cosignatory on something . . . I honestly can't remember. I'm sorry," Jordan said. "Anything else?"

"No," Kate said. "You've been very helpful."

Chapter Fourteen

Kate hung up the telephone and sighed. It was obvious that at least one of the Lawsons had been a crook, but which one? Junius had said Matt, Matt wasn't saying anything, and Jordan sounded like she didn't know. But meanwhile, LuAnne was anxiously waiting for her to return, and depending on the outcome of the signature comparison, the whole speculation about the Lawsons could be moot.

Kate went into the studio, pulled out the folder she'd compiled on the Bixby-house affair, and took out the copy of the canceled check she'd gotten from Emma. She looked at that distinctive signature, "John Matthews," then brought it back into the kitchen and put it, along with Amanda's cards, back in her purse.

The telephone rang again, making Kate jump. "Hello?" she answered.

"Hello, Kate?"

"Amanda?" Kate said, incredulously. "Where are you?"

"I'm at the hospital," she said, "but the doctor says I can come home today."

"Today?" Kate exclaimed, winded. Too much was happening at the same time.

"Yes," Amanda said. "And I was wondering if perhaps you or your husband could come pick me up?"

"Of course. How wonderful. Paul would be happy to come get you."

"Are you sure?"

"Of course I'm sure," Kate said. "I'll send him right up. He should be down at the diner. He'll be up soon. We're looking forward to having you back."

Kate hung up the phone, gathered everything together again, and raced back out to her car. She had to tell Paul to get Amanda, she had to compare signatures with LuAnne and she had to let everyone know that Amanda was coming home.

Kate drove to the diner, parked her car, and hurried inside. Paul was still there, finishing a plate of popcorn shrimp. LuAnne looked at her, wide eyed, as Kate raced to her.

"I've got it, LuAnne!" She pulled the papers out of her purse, then went over to Paul's table and said breathlessly, "I just got a call from Amanda. She's getting out of the hospital this afternoon. I told her you'd go get her."

"How wonderful," Paul said. "I'd be happy to get her. But sit down and catch your breath, Kate. You look like you've been running all over town."

"I have," she said, then went back over to LuAnne and said, "Now, show me the registration."

LuAnne pulled it out of her apron pocket. "Here."

Kate pulled out the check copy and the two women

bent over them. The signatures weren't even close; the handwriting was entirely different. Kate put her arm around LuAnne and hugged her, saying, "It's all right."

Tears rolled down LuAnne's cheeks. "Oh, thank God," she said. "Thank God."

"Amen," Kate agreed. "I'm so glad. Now, you show that registration to Emma when she gets back and make her compare it to her check copies, okay?"

"Oh yes, I will," LuAnne assured her, wiping her eyes. "What a wonderful day this has turned out to be."

Paul came up and paid his bill. "That was delicious, LuAnne. I'm so glad about the signatures. I've got to get going now. Will you make sure my wife gets something to eat?"

"I sure will," LuAnne said. "And it'll be on me."

As Paul was leaving, he heard her say to Kate, "Now you just sit down and tell me what you want for lunch."

"I don't have time," Kate said. "I should head over to Amanda's right now to make sure everything is ready for her to come home."

"Yes, you do," LuAnne replied. "It's one o'clock and you haven't had a thing to eat yet."

Kate suddenly felt faint and sat down on a stool. "Well, maybe a sandwich," she said.

"Grilled cheese," LuAnne said stoutly. "Extra bacon."

Kate nodded her agreement.

"And a slice of rhubarb pie," LuAnne added, smiling.

HALF AN HOUR LATER, Kate was standing at Amanda's, holding the door open for Dot Bagley as she walked in under a flotilla of balloons. Behind her was Martha Sinclair, carrying a vase of daisies.

"I picked these up from Hamilton Road Florist," Martha said. "To welcome her home. I'm sure there'll be lots more coming later on. I always think daisies are so cheerful, don't you?"

"They're some of my favorites," Kate replied.

Dot took the balloons into the living room and looked around for something to tie them to. Finally she just tied them to the leg of the coffee table.

"Good," Martha said. "That way they won't be up on the ceiling. Lots of folks said they would be bringing meals by for Amanda."

"Yes," Kate said. "And Loretta Sweet said she was going to make a batch of cream puffs."

Dot moaned with delight. "Oh, what heaven! Have you ever had those?"

Kate shook her head.

"They're light as air," Dot continued. "We've been trying to get Loretta to put them on the menu for years, but she won't."

"She'd never have time to make anything else if she did," Martha said, her eyes glazing over at the thought.

There was a knock at the door and Kate held it open for Emma Blount, who was carrying a white cake box.

"I heard you went to Pine Ridge this morning," Kate said, trying to be subtle about her concern for Emma's health. "Is everything okay?"

"The doctor says everything will be fine." Emma

sighed, then lifted the cake box toward Kate. "Is there room in the freezer?"

"I believe so. I'll get the door for you," Kate said, following Emma.

The cake just fit into the freezer compartment after Kate took out the ice-cube trays and rearranged some bags of frozen vegetables. She wasn't sure what Amanda would do with an entire ice-cream cake, but she knew everyone was contributing what they could on such short notice to show Amanda that she was loved.

"Perfect," Emma said.

"Yoo-hoo!" Renee Lambert called from the doorway.

Renee was wearing pink from head to toe, including pink, satin high heels. A massive rhinestone brooch dangled from her white pique collar, bracelets jangled on her arms, and her freshly manicured fingers were covered with rings.

"Hi, Renee," Martha called.

Renee sat down in the most comfortable armchair, pulling Kisses out of her shoulder bag and onto her lap. From the way she settled in, Kate felt sure that Renee was planning on staying right there until Amanda arrived. Kisses stretched out his head and snuffled at a balloon that bounced toward him.

"Oh, you see the balloons, don't you, my Little Umpkins? You like balloons, don't you?" Renee pulled a balloon out of the bunch and was waving it in front of Kisses' nose. Kisses sneezed, then barked once. "That's right. That's right, my Little Umpkins." Renee twirled the balloon again and Kisses got up and barked again, his tail wagging, his eyes bright. "By the way," Renee said, "There's a ton of food out in my car, if someone would go get it."

"Sure," Martha said. "Come on, Dot." Emma, who didn't like small dogs, rolled her eyes and went over to the bookcase, where she started looking through the books and magazines.

"Would you like me to come?" Kate asked but stopped as Emma reached out and caught Kate's elbow.

"Look at this!" Emma hissed. Her face had turned red and her hand, which was holding an old, small green book, was trembling with anger.

"What is it?" Kate asked.

"Wordsworth!" Emma said emphatically. "Remember? I told you about the book of poetry I used to read? The one that was missing from Mama's?"

"Oh my goodness. Is that it?" Kate asked.

"It is indeed." Emma opened the book and showed Kate the frontispiece. Written in pale ink with old-fashioned handwriting was "Icey Thompson, 1887." "That's my great-aunt Icey. It was her book and she gave it to Mama."

Martha walked back inside carrying a small Tupperware container.

"That's ham," Renee said.

"Where did you find it?" Kate asked Emma.

Behind her came Dot with another Tupperware container. "And rhubarb cobbler," Renee said.

"Any more?" Kate asked as Dot walked past her on her way to the kitchen. Martha rolled her eyes and shook her head silently.

"No, that's it," Renee said, watching Kisses run around the room, chasing the balloon.

"It was right here in this bookcase," Emma continued, in a low voice, "with these other old books. As soon as I saw it, I knew it was Mama's. But how did it get here?" She looked perplexed.

Kate took the book and leafed through it. *What if Amanda is guilty of the petty thefts after all?* Stuck in between the pages, at "Lucy Gray," was a note. Kate opened the note and read what appeared to be the beginning of a poem, written on plain paper in a bold, black handwriting that looked awfully familiar to Kate: "A violet by a mossy stone . . ." *The same handwriting . . . but no signature.*

"You don't think that Amanda . . . ?" Emma let her voice trail off.

Kate shook her head, ruffling through the pages of the book, hoping to find something else. "I think the same person who stole this from your mother also stole her money." Kate pointed. "Look at the handwriting."

"Oh," Emma said, squinting at the page.

"And that's not Amanda's." Kate glanced at Emma and asked, "By the way, did Lu—"

"Yes," Emma interrupted hastily. "LuAnne showed me the registration," she whispered. "I . . . I apologized. I don't know—"

"What are you two whispering about over there?" Renee demanded.

Kate held up the poetry book. "Wordsworth, Renee. Wonderful poetry. Here, listen." Kate began to read "Lucy Gray," but a tremendous bang interrupted her and startled everyone. Kisses barked furiously at the spot where a balloon had been, then he began looking for it.

"Oh, isn't he precious!" Renee cried. "Come here, my Little Umpkins! Come to Mama!"

Martha shook her head as Kate laid the green book on the hall table.

"Well, I've got to run back to the shop," Emma announced. "Anne's watching things, but the kids will be out of school any minute and things will be hopping."

"Thanks for the cake," Kate said.

"My pleasure," Emma replied. "And I'll drop by later tonight with some chicken."

"Now, you know a heart patient has no business eating fried chicken," Renee said. Kisses had stopped looking for the balloon and was snuffling at Kate's feet. "Come here, my Little Umpkins!"

"Chicken salad," Emma said.

"Oh well." Kisses waddled over to Renee, who reached down and pulled the Chihuahua up into her arms. "All white meat, I hope?"

"Of course," Emma said, shaking her head. "See y'all later."

"I've never gotten over that time someone put dark meat in the chicken salad," Renee said as Emma scooted out the door.

"I've got red beans and rice in the Crock-Pot to bring over later," Dot said.

"And I'm going to make a sweet-potato casserole," Martha added.

"Both sound wonderful," Kate said.

A car door slammed outside and Renee craned her head, trying to see who it was.

"It's Sam Gorman," Martha said.

Renee sniffed.

"And he's got Skip Spencer with him."

"Skip!" Renee exclaimed. "What on earth is he doing with that tomfool deputy?"

"They're pretty friendly," Kate said without mentioning the Copper Mill Players. That was still a deep, dark secret as far as the community and the summer concert series went. She wondered, hoped, that now that Emma had apologized, the Beauty Shop Quartet would be back on track.

"I don't see why anybody talks to that young whipper-snapper," Renee complained. "After he arrested me for picking Joe Tucker's pocket, when all I was trying to do was straighten the poor man's handkerchief." She quivered with indignation.

"That was a long time ago, Renee," Martha reminded her.

"I'll never get over the humiliation. I don't know how he can look me in the face."

"Well, he won't have to try," Martha added. "He's driving off. I think he just gave something to Sam."

Kate smiled as Sam Gorman came in, carrying flowers and a box of candy.

"Hello ladies," he said. "Amanda's not home yet?"

"Not yet," Kate replied. "What lovely flowers."

Sam smiled. "Just a little something for a beautiful lady. And candy from the sheriff and his deputies."

"Well, that was awfully sweet of them," Renee said as if she were the hostess and the recipient. "I'm surprised there aren't more flowers here yet."

"Well, word just got out," Dot said.

"And I'm sure Junius will be here soon with his," Martha said.

Renee flushed and gave Martha a deadly look.

"I mean," Martha added, suddenly confused, "I'm sure a lot of people will be by later on."

But now Kate understood why Renee was parked on that chair like a queen bee. She was waiting all right, but not for Amanda.

Another car door slammed. "Now who's that?" Renee asked, sitting up straighter in the chair.

"It's Betty Anderson," Martha said. "And she's got a pan of something."

Betty, owner of Betty's Beauty Parlor, walked in, and Kisses, who had gone to sleep in Renee's arms, suddenly woke up and started barking.

"I can't stay but a minute," Betty said. "I've got Mabel Trout setting with a permanent, but I wanted to bring this by for Amanda." She handed the dish to Kate as Kisses jumped down and came running up to Betty, barking furiously. "It's a pineapple upside-down cake," Betty said loudly.

"Oh, she'll love it," Kate assured her. "I'll just pop it in the kitchen."

"Well, I made it last night, thinking it would keep, and when Dot called, I was so glad I made it ahead of time."

Kate noticed Sam edging toward the door.

"Thanks for coming by, Sam," she said, smiling.

"Oh," Sam exclaimed, "I almost forgot. I found these two cards lying under one of the hydrangeas outside." He handed Kate the same cards she'd been carrying all morning.

"I swear I've been dropping cards all over town today," she said, sighing. "Thank you."

Sam waved and left.

"I really should go too," Betty said, starting to move off.

Kate turned to the hall table, setting the two cards on top of the others she had brought. She squinted at the one on top. That handwriting looked familiar . . .

"Hey," Betty said, turning back toward Renee. "Can I see that ring?"

Black, bold handwriting . . .

"Which one?" Renee asked.

"The one on the middle finger of your right hand."

It had to be the same. Kate slipped the card into the poetry book and turned around to look at Renee and Betty.

Renee was looking at her hand, at a small silver ring set with turquoise. "Lovely, isn't it?" Renee asked with satisfaction.

"Yes," Betty said. "I think . . . Would you mind taking it off for a moment?"

"Why?" Renee asked sharply.

"Because I think it's mine."

PAUL DROVE BACK from Pine Ridge carefully. Beside him, Amanda was gazing out the window with that intense rapture he had seen so often on the faces of hospital patients who were finally allowed outside again. It was a beautiful sunny day, with white clouds floating lazily across a perfectly blue sky and flowers whose colors looked more brilliant against the green trees. He glanced at Amanda and smiled to himself. Someone in the hospital had plaited her hair into two braids, which gave her a piquant appearance, almost of a little girl playing grown-up.

Amanda must have felt his gaze, because she turned her face toward him and smiled, saying, "What a beautiful day! I'm so happy to be going home."

"We've all missed you," Paul said. "And we're all glad you're okay."

They rode on in silence for a while and then Amanda said, "You know, I've been spending a lot of time thinking. Of course, there's not much else to do in a hospital besides think."

Paul chuckled.

"Last night, I was thinking about how many mistakes you can make in life. And yet, somehow, it all turns out. I've always believed in the providence of God. Or rather, I've always thought I believed in it, but I can see now that I didn't fully. There were things I couldn't understand, so I thought that meant that somehow God wasn't involved."

"If we could understand everything, we wouldn't need grace," Paul said quietly.

Amanda nodded. "I'm such a slow learner," she said

with a delicate laugh. "I'm just now seeing for the first time that God really is involved in everything. He'll work it all out. There's always hope." She stopped and laughed again. "But what am I telling you all this for? You're the pastor."

"But I can never hear it too often," Paul said. "We all need to be reminded of how much God loves us."

"Well," Amanda said thoughtfully. "That makes me feel better."

They drove through Copper Mill slowly and pulled up outside of Amanda's house.

"My," she said, "There are a lot of cars."

"You're popular," Paul said cheerfully, although he was frustrated. What Amanda undoubtedly needed most was rest. He got out of the car and went around and opened the door for her, giving her his arm and helping her out. "Don't worry about your things," he said. "I'll come back and get them in a minute."

Amanda nodded and they made their way slowly up the walk. When they reached the door, Paul's vague disappointment changed into appalled consternation as angry voices reached them.

"Yes, it is!"

"No, it isn't!"

Paul and Amanda glanced at each other, and he saw Amanda straighten her shoulders and reach for the doorknob.

They walked inside to see Betty and Renee faced off furiously under streamers of crepe paper.

"Yes, it is!"

"Enough!" Paul boomed, surprising everyone into silence. "What's going on here?"

Kate came running forward. "Amanda. Here, come and sit down." She took Amanda's arm and helped her over to the sofa.

Betty took a deep breath and said, "Renee is wearing a ring I lost."

"It's not the—" Renee began, but Paul interrupted her.

"This is not the time or place—" Paul began, but Renee interrupted him.

"It's not the same one," Renee snapped. "It can't be. It was a present. I received it as a present," she insisted, her eyes filling with tears. "None of you may believe me, but I did!" She snatched her shoulder bag, swept Kisses into her arms, and marched out the front door.

"Well," Betty said, looking around uncomfortably. Her cheeks were flushed. "I'd better get going too. I'm so glad you're home, Amanda. I'm sorry . . ."

"Nonsense," Amanda said with quiet dignity. "And thank you for coming by."

"What on earth was going on?" Paul asked Kate quietly as Martha and Dot both welcomed Amanda home.

"I'll tell you later," Kate replied.

"It was so kind of you to bring all this food," Amanda said, smiling gallantly, but her voice was heavy with exhaustion.

"You're quite welcome," Dot said. "We'll be on our way now."

"Yes, you look worn out," Martha said, then she flushed as she always did when she realized she'd spoken a bit too frankly. "I mean, what with being in the hospital and all."

"Well, thank you for all your trouble," Amanda replied graciously.

"No trouble at all," Dot said.

As Dot and Martha left, Paul came back in with Amanda's things. "Where would you like these?"

"Oh, in my bedroom," Amanda said.

"Would you like me to help you unpack them?" Kate asked.

"That would be lovely, dear," Amanda replied. "But first, how about a nice cup of tea?"

"I'll put the kettle on," Kate said. "You sit and rest."

"I need to get going," Paul said. "I've got to look in at the church and see if there are any messages for me."

"You go right ahead," Amanda told him. "I appreciate your bringing me home."

In the bedroom Kate helped Amanda change into a fresh nightgown. By the time Amanda had opened all of her mail and read the get-well cards she had received, the kettle was boiling and Kate poured a pot of tea.

"The tea is steeping," Kate said, coming back into the bedroom. "Where shall I put your things?"

"Don't worry about them," Amanda said wearily. "Just set my purse down by the side of the bureau. And if you'd get out my wallet and checkbook from the bureau drawer and put them in my purse, that would be nice."

Kate opened the bureau drawer and pulled out the wallet and checkbook. She glanced back at Amanda, whose eyes were half shut.

"Oh," Amanda said, rousing herself. "Would you dig out a twenty from the stack there for the boy who mows my lawn? He's bound to stop by sooner or later. I see he's kept my grass cut while I was gone."

"You mean from your wallet?" Kate asked. She hadn't seen any money in the drawer, neither this time nor the time she'd looked before.

"No, the money in drawer," Amanda said. Her voice was sounding fainter and fainter. "My secret stash. It might be under the gray gloves."

Kate's heart skipped a beat as she quickly rifled through the gloves and scarves. No money was there. Kate opened Amanda's wallet. There was no cash in it either. Kate glanced in the mirror at Amanda lying in bed with her eyes closed.

Kate thought swiftly. Junius had advised Amanda to take her wallet and checkbook out of her purse and put them in her bureau drawer. Kate could see it clearly: Junius seeing the stash of money. The gleam of greed in his eyes. Taking Amanda to her car and telling her that he needed to run back into the house for some reason, maybe to make sure everything was turned off. It would only take a moment.

Kate glanced back at Amanda and noticed that her eyes were still closed. She closed the drawer quietly and went over to Amanda. She was sound asleep.

Kate looked over at the bedside table where Amanda had placed the stack of cards that had come in the mail, and she noticed another card with the familiar handwriting. She picked up the card and envelope, walked out of the bedroom into the living room, and pulled the other card out of the volume of Wordsworth. The same bold black handwriting . . . Kate hesitated for a moment.

She fingered the get-well card, then flipped it open. Under the printed get-well message was a short note:

> Wishing you the best, now and always.
> Love,
> Junius

Chapter Fifteen

K ate looked at the card and pulled out the other evidence: The big black *J* in "Junius" matched the *J* of the name "John" on the check copy and the handwriting of all of the cards—the poetry-book note included—was identical. She sighed with satisfaction, as well as sadness. Junius, that wonderful dancer, that polished gentleman, that delightful social butterfly had been transformed into a thief. Her mouth hardened. It was time to come to a reckoning with Mr. Lawson.

Gathering up all her evidence, she headed impulsively toward the door, only to stop short. Amanda was asleep; did she dare leave her alone? Should she call someone? Then she heard a car door outside and, looking out the window, saw Patricia Harris coming up the walk, with Joe Tucker behind her.

Thanking God with all her heart, Kate ran outside. "Oh, I'm so glad you're here!"

"Why, what is it?" Patricia asked. "Is Amanda all right?"

"She's fine," Kate said breathlessly. "But she's taking a nap and I really need to go somewhere. Could you sit with her for a while, Patricia?"

"Of course," Patricia replied. "I'd be happy to."

After Patricia had gone inside, Joe turned to Kate and asked, "All right, what's happened?"

Kate didn't hesitate. Joe was a man she could trust absolutely, and besides, he loved Amanda and would do anything he could to help her. "Amanda's been robbed."

Joe started to speak, but Kate put a hand on his arm. "She doesn't know it yet. But I've got to find Junius. Do you know where he lives?"

"Sure do," Joe said, walking toward Kate's car. "You can fill me in as we go."

JUNIUS LIVED IN A SET of apartments at the junction of Smoky Mountain Road and Smith Street, south of town. In the few minutes it took to drive there, Kate talked as fast as she could, cramming in as much information in as little time as possible: Ada Blount, the checks, the petty thefts, the lawsuit, the cards. As they pulled into the apartment complex, Kate was still talking.

"And when I saw that Amanda's money was gone, I knew that the only person who could have stolen it was Junius. He was the only one who saw her secret stash. I compared the handwriting on the card and the canceled check, and they're the same. We've got to find him."

Joe looked around the parking lot. "His car isn't here. You stay in the car and I'll go knock on his door."

He got out of the car, walked up to apartment 1B, and knocked loudly. Kate sat watching him, her fingers crossed. What if Junius had left town? She watched as Joe peered into the windows, then shook his head. He came back to the car and got in.

"He's not there."

Kate let out an exasperated sigh.

"I'll tell you what. He wasn't at the diner this morning either. And he didn't show up for deliveries at the Bixby house. I thought he might be sick. I was going to check on him later, but now . . . I think he's run off."

"Matt," Kate said firmly. "Matt will know where he is."

She looked at her watch. A quarter to four. "He'll still be at the bank," she said, backing out of the parking space. "Oh, Joe,"—she pulled onto Smith Street—"what am I going to tell him?"

"The truth," Joe said. "That whole lawsuit thing sounds like he already knows. Just doesn't want to admit it. How did that end up, anyway?"

Kate sighed. "Matt wrote a settlement check. Restitution. That's what had me confused for a while. I wasn't sure whether Matt was the guilty one."

"Meanwhile, there's Emma thinking it was LuAnne's husband."

Kate glanced quickly at Joe, who gave her a rueful look.

She parked outside the bank and the two went inside, passing the perking coffee pot and the hovering Mr. McKinney, and only waving at the Cline sisters as they headed straight for Matt's cubicle. Matt looked up from his laptop as they walked in.

"Mrs. Hanlon, Mr. Tucker," he said. "What can I do for you?"

"You can tell us where your dad might be," Joe said. "We need to talk to him."

"What about?" Matt asked.

"This," Kate said. With shaking hands, she pulled out the pieces of evidence from her purse and laid them on the desk in front of Matt. "This is the copy of the endorsement on the back of one of the checks Ada Blount wrote to cash."

"John Matthews," Matt read in a voice that sounded like an echo.

"And I just left Amanda's," Kate continued. "She's been robbed of a significant amount of cash and I think . . . no, I know that your father is the only one who could have done it."

Kate waited for a reaction and then chided herself for doing so. Matt wasn't going to react normally, if at all. She had to quit expecting that of him. "Matt, where is your father?"

"I don't know," he said. His eyes were still riveted on the check. "John Matthews."

"Yes," Kate said. "You recognize that name, don't you? He used it in Asheville, didn't he?"

Matt's eyes flickered toward her, then away. He nodded slowly but didn't say a word. "Matt, where is he?"

"The checks, the money, the card." Matt sounded like he was making a list. "Yesterday was payday. Was she missing any credit cards?" he asked.

"I don't know," Kate said incredulously.

"She probably is," Matt said, still looking at the papers. "At least one."

"Matt, where is he?" Joe asked. "Where do you think he went?"

Matt looked up toward Joe and said, "Probably back to North Carolina. Cherokee. He cashed his pension check yesterday. He usually goes to the casino in Cherokee and gambles until it's gone. If he's got a credit card, it'll take longer."

"Cherokee?" Joe asked.

Matt nodded.

Joe turned to Kate. "Let's go."

Kate began to gather up the papers on Matt's desk.

"You're going after him?" Matt asked.

"Yep," Joe said curtly.

Matt turned off his laptop and stood up. "I'll come with you."

Kate glanced at Joe. "It's quite a drive."

"He's my dad."

Joe looked at him for a moment, then nodded. "Okay."

"I'll be the navigator," Matt offered as they walked toward Kate's car. "I'm good with maps."

"I'll bet you are, Son," Joe said, clapping Matt on the back.

Kate was buckling her seat belt when suddenly the back door opened and a rush of Estée Lauder's Youth-Dew filled the car. Kate gasped and turned around as Renee slid across the backseat and shut the door before anyone could say a word.

"Renee!" Kate exclaimed. "What are you doing?"

"Going with you," Renee snapped, clicking her seat belt. "Don't crush Kisses," she told Joe, who had recoiled against the door.

"Renee, you can't . . . Where do you think we're going?" Kate asked.

"To find Junius, of course," Renee said. "Well, I want to find him too. I have a few questions for that man." She flung back her head defiantly and crossed her arms.

Kate and Joe exchanged helpless glances.

"We can't take the dog," Joe said, looking at the little Chihuahua, who was already settling himself down to sleep with the asthmatic snorts that Kate knew from experience would soon be loud snoring.

"Nonsense," Renee said. "Kisses will be no trouble at all."

"It's a two-hour trip," Joe said.

"Actually, three," Matt corrected. "If you keep to the posted speed limit."

"Three," Joe agreed. "And that's without stops."

"Then I suggest we get going," Renee replied firmly.

Kate hastily started the car and backed out of the parking space in front of the bank. She knew when she was beaten.

"Turn on Smith Street for zero point one miles to Main Street, then turn left and go east one point two miles to I-40 east," Matt advised.

"I know how to get to I-40, Matt," Kate said. "But thank you."

Kate glanced down at the slightly stubby cell-phone-like device in Matt's hands. "What on earth is that?"

"My BlackBerry," he said. "It has wireless e-mail, Internet, Bluetooth technology, speaker phone, personal organizer, text and instant messaging, and GPS."

Kate nodded. She'd heard of the device but had no idea why it seemed to be so vital to businesspeople. "That's good," she said.

"Yes," Matt agreed eagerly. "With the assisted GPS—that stands for Global Positioning System—I can get driving instructions and update them in real time, so even if we make a wrong turn, I can get alternative directions instantly."

"So where are we headed?" Renee asked, stroking Kisses.

"Casino," Joe said. "Junius seems to be a gambler. That right, Son?" he asked Matt.

Matt didn't respond, so Joe tapped his shoulder.

"Huh?"

"Your dad. You said he liked to gamble."

Matt nodded.

"Maybe you'd better tell us what you can about your dad," Kate said to Matt as she pulled onto I-40 east.

Matt looked up from his BlackBerry and sighed. "He's been a gambler for as long as I can remember. Mom and Dad fought all the time about money. I didn't understand then, but later, when I was in junior high, he . . . I'm good with figures," he explained. "When Dad found out, he asked me to work out these algorithms. It was so he could make bets scientifically. You need a lot of information to work out an algorithm for, like, a horse race. Football was easier. I could do football."

Kate remembered Junius' version of Matt's childhood. "Did he bet on the high-school football games?" Kate asked.

Matt nodded. "Big time. When it came out, there was a huge fight. Mom made me promise never to help him with his bets again. She told me it was a crime. I'd never realized it was wrong before," he explained.

"Well, I never!" Renee exclaimed. "Didn't know?"

"Hush," Joe said, nodding toward the front seat.

Renee lowered her voice slightly. "How can you *not* know?"

"So you never did it again," Kate said.

"No. Mom told me not to," Matt said simply. "After that, Dad left."

"Where did he go?" Kate asked.

"I don't know, but he ended up in Asheville," Matt said. "Mom and I were still in Gainesville, Georgia."

"That's the accent," Renee said proudly. "I knew it wasn't North Carolina, no matter what Junius said. Georgia."

Kate ignored Renee and asked, "When did you and your Dad get back in touch?"

"After Mom died," Matt said. "He came to the funeral and said he'd wanted to stay in touch with me, but Mom wouldn't let him." Matt almost looked Kate in the eyes. "Do you think that was true?"

"I don't know, Matt," Kate said.

"I wasn't sure. I'm still not sure. But he wanted to be with me, he said, and Mom had told me to try to help him if I could. So when he asked me to move up to Asheville, I did. He said he had an investment firm and that I could work for him. That way we'd be together. He promised me there'd be no more gambling." Matt blinked a couple of times.

"It's all right, Matt," Kate said, looking at his impassive face out of the corner of her eye. "But I should tell you, I've talked to Jordan Harnett."

"Who's Jordan Harnett?" Renee asked.

"Then you know all about it," Matt said.

"If someone doesn't tell me something soon, I'm going to scream!"

"Now, Renee." Joe tried to calm her down.

"Well, I will," Renee said. "Here this man's been carry-ing on all sorts of—"

"Not all about it, Matt," Kate interrupted. "But enough to know that you nearly went to trial and that you settled it."

"I had to," Matt said.

"Matt," Joe interrupted everyone. "Would you mind telling us what happened before Renee wakes up Kisses with all her squirming and squalling?"

Matt sighed. "I moved to Asheville. Went to work for the firm. After a couple of years, I realized that Dad was embezzling money. It took me that long to catch on, because he had his own clients and I had mine. And the bookkeeper was a friend of his. A lady friend."

"Who was that?" Renee asked sharply.

"Dorothy Lake," Matt said. "I think she moved to Virginia. Anyway, Dad was gambling away most of the profits. Actually,"—Matt turned around toward the backseat and explained—"it was a very intelligent scheme: He took money from the firm and from the other clients and put it into a series of accounts. Very hard to track. Kept transferring it from place to place until it ended up in another account he'd set up under the name John Matthews—"

"John Matthews," Kate interrupted. "Junius' alias."

"I thought he was a client. That's what Dad always said. John Matthews, a special client. A recluse, a man who lives alone and doesn't like to come out and meet people."

"But, in fact, John Matthews was Junius Lawson," Joe said.

Matt nodded.

"What finally made the red light go off?"

"Huh?" Matt asked, bewildered.

"How did you find out about the deception?" Joe asked.

"Oh. It was when Dorothy quit. I think Dad dumped her or something. She was really mad, so she gave me the books. She said I should look them over. I did and I could see where monies had been transferred from one account to another in an inappropriate manner. She told me that these were the real books that she'd kept on the side.

"You know, there were two sets of books. The fake books Dad gave the IRS and me, and these real books that

Dorothy kept so she could have a handle on Dad. I double-checked all of it, of course, but it was all true. So I went to Dad and asked him what was going on. He tried to bluff his way out of it, but I showed him the bank statements and he finally admitted to what he'd done. He had to. I had the figures right there and figures don't lie. I think that's why I like them so much. They're secure. Trustworthy."

"And your father isn't," Joe said.

There was a long pause. "It turned out he'd embezzled about fifty thousand dollars from Mr. Harnett."

"Fifty thousand!" Renee cried.

"Oh, it could have been a lot worse," Matt assured her. "All of it came out just as he was about to liquidate Mr. Donnelly's account and *he* was worth about a quarter of a million. I could never have paid that back."

"Fifty thousand," Renee repeated.

"So that wiped out Mr. . . . uh . . . What was his name?" Joe asked.

"Harnett," Kate answered. "Franklin Harnett. I found the newspaper article that reported on the settlement."

Matt nodded.

"The only question was whether it was you or your father who was guilty . . . or both."

"I'll bet Dad told you I was guilty," Matt said, turning toward Kate.

"He told me a story," Kate said carefully.

Matt turned away and looked out the side window as he said, "He did that before. Back in Asheville, one of our clients came in to complain about his investments and Dad told him that I'd mishandled them. Made a poor investment and lost the lot. The worst part of it was that the client believed him. Everybody believes Dad. He's got . . . something.''

"He's got personality," Renee said.

"Renee!" Kate scolded.

"Well, he does," Renee retorted. "But personality isn't everything. Honesty's a lot better, Matt, and don't you ever forget that. But why on earth didn't you tell everybody this before?"

"He's my dad," Matt said simply.

When they reached Sevierville, Kate stopped to get gas and let everyone stretch their legs. While Renee took Kisses over to a little plot of grass to do his business, Kate used her cell phone to call Paul. There was no answer at home or at the church, so Kate left a message on each answering machine, telling him where she was headed.

"Paul not there?" Joe asked.

"No," Kate said.

"Probably over at Amanda's," Joe replied.

Kate nodded. She wasn't worried about where Paul was. She was worried about what they were going to do once they got to Cherokee. She looked at her posse: Joe and Renee, both elderly, even though Renee would never admit it, and herself and Matt. None of them likely candidates for Junius to listen to, much less obey. How were they going to get Junius back to Copper Mill? Why hadn't she thought this out instead of just taking off like that?

Kate pulled out her phone and dialed.

"Amanda?" Joe asked.

Kate shook her head. "Sheriff Roberts."

Joe raised his eyebrows.

"Sheriff's office."

"Rosalie? This is Kate Hanlon. Is Sheriff Roberts there? It's urgent."

"Just a moment, Mrs. Hanlon," Rosalie replied. She could hear Rosalie whisper something to somebody.

"Kate." Alan Roberts' voice came on the line. "What can I do for you?"

Kate took a deep breath and began the long explanation of why she was pursuing Junius Lawson. Sheriff Roberts listened silently. "So, you see, I'm not quite sure what to do when we get there," she concluded.

"I don't think there's anything you can do," Sheriff Roberts replied. "Why didn't you come to me with the evidence and let me deal with it? You say you have evidence?"

"Yes, I have evidence. So does Emma Blount. She's got copies of the canceled checks. And you can talk to Amanda."

"Believe me, I will. I was going over there later anyway. And you say Matt's with you?"

"Yes," Kate replied.

"I'll need to talk to him too."

"But meanwhile, Junius is in Cherokee, North Carolina."

"You mean you think he's in Cherokee," the sheriff corrected.

"Well, that's where Matt says he always goes." Kate was beginning to wish she hadn't called. "Is there anything you can do to help us out?"

There was a long silence.

"Well," Sheriff Roberts finally said, "none of this is proper procedure, but I'll call Sheriff Granville over in Cherokee and ask him to meet you at the casino. I'm not sure what he can do; the jurisdiction's complicated by tribal law. This number you're using, is it a public telephone or your cell phone?"

"My cell." Kate gave him the number.

"Somebody will call you. If not Granville, then me."

"Thank you," Kate said gratefully.

"You're welcome," Sheriff Roberts said and hung up.

Chapter Sixteen

Half an hour later, they turned onto Route 441 and into the Great Smoky Mountains National Park. The road was a thin ribbon of asphalt that wound through the towering mountains. Sheer cliffs and long rock slides, from where the road had originally been blasted, alternated with thick, untouched forest. Here and there a mountain stream plunged down a cliff, running through a culvert under the road to come out the other side and race down yet another cliff. Birds darted back and forth before them, while hawks played on the thermals high overhead. It was all absolutely beautiful, but Kate wished that someone else was driving so she could enjoy it. Each spectacular vista meant riding a knife edge, with a slim guard rail between themselves and a chasm, whose bottom she certainly couldn't see.

"What time is it?" she asked, her hands gripping the steering wheel tightly. Long shadows were spreading across the road.

"Six twenty three," Matt said. He hadn't been paying attention to the scenery or the road, but had kept his eyes fixed on the GPS map on his BlackBerry the whole time.

"It shouldn't be getting dark this early," she exclaimed.

"It's the mountains," Joe said. "Always gets darker a little earlier up here."

"Look! Deer!" Renee called.

Kate didn't dare look. All her concentration was centered on the endless succession of switchbacks and drop-offs.

Kate's phone rang as they came out of the mountains and into the outskirts of Cherokee. She quickly pulled into a gas station and answered.

"I talked with Sheriff Granville," Sheriff Roberts said without preamble. "He said when you get to the casino, you should go talk to John Henderson. He's in charge of security. He'll help you out."

"John Henderson. All right," Kate replied.

"By the way," the sheriff continued. "I talked to Emma Blount. She confirmed your story about Ada's money. Showed me the checks. Definitely talk to Henderson before you do anything else. A man in Lawson's shoes might be feeling a bit desperate and you never know what a desperate man will do."

THE CASINO LOOKED LIKE a small lodge, mostly because the adjoining hotel was fifteen stories tall. But as the four of them walked in, they were dwarfed by the forty-foot-tall entrance. They walked between the massive stone pillars that held up a network of wooden beams over a

walkway done in a Native American basketry design. And
then they stepped into the casino proper and looked out at
an endless sea of gaming machines, all of them beeping,
blipping, or ringing, their lights flashing, racing, pulsing.

Kate felt overwhelmed. She glanced over at Joe, who
looked as stunned and bewildered as she felt. Matt, on the
other hand, simply scanned the crowd. She glanced past
him to Renee, who was craning her head in all directions.

"Let's go find Mr. Henderson," Kate said, recovering
her wits at last.

But where to start . . . There didn't seem to be any
security around. The group wandered through the aisles
for a bit, then asked a cocktail waitress, who directed
them to the customer-service desk.

"Can I help you?" asked a young Native American
woman with long, straight jet-black hair and warm brown
eyes. The nametag clipped to her white oxford-style shirt
said Rhoda.

"We're trying to find John Henderson," Kate said. "We
understand he's with security?"

"Yes, he is," the young woman replied, a worried look
on her face. "Is there a problem?"

"There might be," Kate said. "If you could tell us
where we could find him?"

"I'll call him," Rhoda said. "Please, have a seat."

Kate and Joe sat down on a couple of tan chairs tucked
into the recessed corner and waited. Renee placed Kisses
on her lap, while Matt paced up and down the room.
People came and went around them, a few stopping to cash

in their winnings. Beyond them, the casino pulsated with lights and noise. It was beginning to give Kate a headache. She watched as an elderly lady in a navy suit stopped at the service desk, a short, nondescript man behind her.

Matt leaned toward Kate and said, "I hope he doesn't take too long. I'm getting hungry."

"Mrs. Hanlon?"

Kate looked up at the nondescript man and said, "Yes."

"John Henderson," he said, sitting down next to her. "I talked to Sheriff Granville earlier. It sounds like we might have a thief in the place."

"Yes," Kate replied. "Junius Lawson."

"He's my dad," Matt added.

"Sorry to hear that," Henderson said. "You wouldn't happen to have a photograph of him, would you?"

Matt reached for his wallet, pulled out a photograph of Junius, and handed it to him. Henderson took it and looked at it for a minute.

"I know him," Henderson said. "He's a high roller. He had car trouble last time he was up here and I sent Bob out to help him. But he didn't use the name Lawson. Matthews. That was the name he gave." Henderson shrugged. "Lots of fake names around here. You mind if I show it to the cashiers?"

Matt and Kate shook their heads.

"Back in a minute."

"He doesn't seem too upset," Kate commented.

Matt shook his head. Once again Kate reminded herself that Matt didn't understand small talk.

Henderson returned with the photograph and gave it back to Matt. "They scanned it and sent it to all our security personnel on their cells. Someone will spot him if he's here."

"Did any of the cashiers remember him?" Kate asked.

"Denise did. She cashed a check for him about a month ago. A couple of thousand, made out to cash. She remembered it because it was a third-party check and she had to get special permission from the manager." Henderson shrugged again. "He's a high roller. They get special favors."

Henderson looked at them and grimaced. "This may take a while. Stay here and I'll let you know what's going on."

Kate nodded.

"Don't worry. We'll find him." Henderson winked at her and walked out to the main room of the casino.

Everyone in the group tried to be patient, but with only the beige walls to look at, they soon began to get restless.

"What on earth is taking them so long?" Renee asked. "What time is it, Kate?"

"It's seven thirty," Kate said. "We only got here an hour ago."

"They should have caught him by now." Renee looked around. "I think we should go find him."

"Mr. Henderson asked us to stay put and wait for him to come back," Kate said.

"Fiddle-faddle. I didn't come all this way just to sit," Renee said scrambling out of her seat.

She picked up her shoulder bag, jostling Kisses awake enough so that he stopped snoring. "Come on, Kisses. Let's go find the bad man."

"Renee!" Kate got up. "Please, let's just wait."

"Nonsense! I'm not the type to sit around and wait for things to happen." Renee turned on her heel and marched off, clutching her handbag and Kisses.

"Come on, guys," Kate said, sighing. "Let's go after her."

The three of them followed Renee, emerging from the relative quiet of the service area into the cacophony of the casino. Renee was standing at the entrance, looking out at the cavernous space.

"Well, where shall we go, Renee?" Kate asked.

Renee glanced at her with a strange expression in her eyes. "Maybe we should all split up and take a section. Divide the search," she suggested.

"We do that, we'll never find each other again," Joe said. "This place is as big as Bristol Caverns. And I bet it'd be about as dark, if you switched off the lights."

"Joe's right," Kate said. "If we're going to look for Junius ourselves, we need to stick together."

The four headed into the casino proper. People were at every machine, lights were flashing, the beeps and blips sounding. As they walked down the endless aisles, Kate looked as carefully as she could at every tall, white-haired man they passed. In this crowd, there were quite a few. Renee trotted along, a few steps ahead, slowing down occasionally to peer at someone but always moving on. At one station, an elderly lady about Renee's size suddenly jumped up and down as her machine exploded in a flurry of lights and music.

"I won!" the woman cried. "I won!"

A crowd gathered, among them another nondescript man with a cell phone and something else clipped to his belt. *Security*, Kate thought, proud of herself for recognizing the equipment. She glanced over at Renee, who had stopped to watch along with everyone else.

"I wonder how much she won," Kate said to Renee.

Renee looked away but not before Kate had seen the wide-eyed look on her face. Kate sighed as they all went on again. The place was huge. How would they find anybody in there?

They turned down a long aisle of penny slots, and Kate tried to focus and keep from letting the blinking lights distract her. As they neared the end of the row, she heard a voice she recognized coming from around the corner.

"It's perfectly fine, I tell you," a man said. "It's my wife's credit card. She's in the ladies room. She'll be back in a minute."

Before Kate realized what was going on, Renee had whirled around and yelled, "Junius Lawson! You skunk!"

The white-haired man froze just long enough for Renee to set her shoulder bag on the floor and hiss, "Sic 'em, Kisses!"

Kate watched, too astounded to move, as Kisses leaped out of the shoulder bag and went charging through the myriad feet, straight toward Junius. Junius snatched something out of the hostess' hand and started walking away from them as swiftly as he could.

"Dad?" Matt called. He glanced at Joe and said, "You cover long and I'll cover short." Then he started barreling his way through the crowd after Junius. "Dad!"

Joe lowered his head and started moving off toward one side in a long arc through the crowd to intercept Junius.

"Mr. Bly!" cried the hostess.

"Go get 'em, Kisses!" Renee hollered, tottering on her pink high heels, her shoulder bag dangling from one hand as she shoved people out of her way with the other.

"Dad!"

Kate found herself shoving her way through the crowd as well, trying to keep an eye on Junius as he ducked and dodged his way toward the front of the casino. The trouble was, there were so many people and so many other white-haired men. It would be easy to lose him. Kate rammed into someone and apologized as she kept moving.

"Junius Lawson! You come right back here!" Renee bawled. "Kisses! Kisses!"

In the midst of all the other noise, Kate could hear the yapping of the little dog she knew so well. She prayed that no one would step on him.

"Dad!"

Kate pushed through another knot of people. In front of her, a man in a white shirt, with something clipped to his belt, was holding a cell phone to his mouth. "Security alert. Security alert. Number 902 headed toward main entrance."

Kate pushed her way forward. Number 902 had to be Junius. Up ahead she could see Matt plowing through the crowd, and over to her right, Joe was determinedly homing in on a tall, white-haired figure. Someone's purse smacked Kate across the chest. Ahead of her, Renee's stiff

blonde curls were coming undone, her ankles were bow-
ing, but she was still going, still determined, still furious,
and still at full volume.

"Junius Lawson! You rotten snake!"

Joe, within arm's length, lunged at Junius, and as
Junius staggered backward to evade him, a dog's
anguished yelp filled the air. Renee leaped forward with
the cry and claws of a tigress. Kate jumped after her and
watched as Renee sprang off the floor and landed on
Junius, knocking him to the floor.

"You lying thief! You heartless coward! You—"

Kate snatched Kisses from the floor and held him to
her chest. Kisses wheezed and shivered as a host of white-
shirted security men appeared and grappled with the two
figures on the floor.

A moment later, Renee came up in the arms of one of
them. She took a deep breath and shook herself free.

"Well, there's the perp," she said, straightening her
clothes. "Haul him away."

"Number 902 apprehended by the Lucky Sevens,"
said one security man standing next to Joe, who was bent
over, wheezing from his exertions.

"Kisses? Where's my Kisses?" Renee cried.

"I've got him, Renee," Kate said, holding up the
Chihuahua.

"Oh, my Little Umpkins," Renee crooned, taking him
from Kate. "Is Mama's Little Umpkins hurt?"

"He's fine, Renee," Kate assured her.

"No thanks to him," Renee said, glaring at Junius.

"Are you all right, Joe?" Kate asked.

Joe nodded.

"This is a huge mistake," Junius said to the security man holding him. He was breathing hard. He gestured toward Renee and said, "This . . . this woman has been stalking me. And I was trying to get away from her."

"Liar," Renee said with withering disdain. "You gave me stolen presents. You've been stealing from everybody!"

"Including an Amanda Bly?" John Henderson had arrived and was looking over the credit card that had been taken from Junius' hand.

"Yes," Kate said, coming forward. "He stole that card from an elderly lady in Tennessee."

Junius looked around, his face changing from exasperation with Renee to rueful regret and embarrassment as his gaze shifted to Kate and Joe, and ending up in cold anger when he saw Matt.

Matt's eyes looked like a whipped puppy's as he said, sadly, "I couldn't let you get away with it again, Dad."

"Mr. Matthews . . . sorry, Mr. Lawson," Henderson said. "I'm afraid we're going to have to hold you until the sheriff gets here."

"On what charge?" Junius asked disdainfully.

"Stolen credit card."

Junius snorted.

Henderson turned to Renee, who was still quivering with anger. "Do you have any charges to file, ma'am?"

"I most certainly do. This man stole this ring"—she took off the tiny silver ring with turquoise settings—"from a friend of mine and gave it to me. And he . . ." Renee stopped and, looking around, caught her breath.

"I understand," Henderson said soothingly. "It's a little too public out here. We'll need to get statements from all of you, so if you would come back to my office. Sheriff Granville should be here any minute." Henderson nodded to the security man holding Junius and he started dragging the older man away.

"You can't hold me like this!" Junius cried. "I'm innocent, I tell you!"

As they followed Henderson, Junius, and the rest of the security personnel, Renee dropped back slightly until she was even with Kate as they neared the customer-service desk.

"Come with me," she whispered to Kate, and then, taking Kate's arm, she called aloud to Henderson, "We'll be right there!" as she pulled Kate into the ladies' room.

Inside, Renee was about to say something else, but she saw herself in the mirror and gasped, "My land! I look like a mud fence with briars in it!"

Setting her shoulder bag on the counter, she dug around Kisses for various items. She pulled out a comb and began working on her stiff curls. Kate simply waited.

After Renee had pulled out a lipstick, she glanced at Kate in the mirror and asked boldly, "How much do you think I should tell this Sheriff Granville?"

"Everything," Kate said.

Renee stopped in midlip and looked at her beseechingly.

"You've got to, Renee. If he gave you any other presents, or if you made any investments . . ."

Suddenly Renee's eyes were wet. She set down her lipstick and blinked the tears back. "I was . . . I was such a fool!"

"Oh, Renee." Kate put her arm around Renee, who turned her head into Kate's shoulder and sobbed for a moment. "It's all right. It's not your fault."

"I know that," Renee said, pulling back and fumbling for a tissue. She wiped her eyes carefully as she said, "It was that skunk, Junius. Doing me a favor. Double my money. Hah!" She threw the tissue away. "Do I really have to tell them?"

"Well," Kate said, "they're probably going to find out anyway. I'm not sure about the—"

Renee interrupted. "Do you think he got any money from Amanda?"

"I have no idea," Kate said. "But I think he was definitely buttering her up to get money out of her. That's his pattern. He gave Ada presents too, you know. And the more proof that's provided, the more likely a jury will believe he's guilty."

"Believe he's guilty?" Renee exclaimed. "He *is* guilty! Guilty as sin! If I thought for one minute that he'd get off—" She picked up her shoulder bag. "I'll tell that sheriff everything, all right," she said. "Come on, Kate. Don't dawdle."

Chapter Seventeen

When Kate woke up the next morning, she stared in disbelief at a clock that said ten thirty. She scrambled out of bed, pulled on her bathrobe, and padded to the kitchen, where she found Paul talking on the telephone.

"Oh, I agree. Providential. Yes, I certainly will tell her as soon as she gets up." He winked at Kate as she poured herself a cup of coffee from the brimming pot. "No. No problem. I'll let her know." He hung up the phone, put an arm around Kate, and kissed her. "Good morning, sleepyhead."

She kissed him back. "Good morning. Almost afternoon. Why didn't you wake me up earlier? Who was that on the phone?"

"You didn't get in until two," Paul replied. "Toast?"

Kate nodded.

"That was Dot Bagley." Paul put two slices of wholewheat bread in the toaster. "She was calling to make sure you were fine and to see if I could fill her in on all the news. She was the tenth call this morning."

Kate looked at him wide-eyed over her coffee cup.

"The jungle drums are pounding all over town." Paul leaned over and kissed the top of her head. "I'm just thankful you're home safe."

"But not alone," Kate reminded him. "I had Joe and Matt with me."

"And Renee," Paul added.

"Yes, well, that wasn't my idea."

"I'm sure." Paul put the toast on a plate and handed it to Kate. "Eat up," he said as she started buttering. "You're going to need your strength. I have a feeling that everyone in the Faith Freezer Program is either going to call or come by to hear the saga straight from the horse's mouth."

Kate groaned and took a big bite of toast. "I've got to get dressed," she said swallowing. "Have you heard from Matt?"

Paul shook his head.

"How's Amanda?"

"Just fine," Paul said. "Sheriff Roberts filled her in last night."

"How did she take it?" Kate asked, taking a large swallow of coffee.

"Quietly furious at Junius. And quietly proud of Joe being part of the posse." He winked at Kate. "There might be a thaw coming."

"Maybe." Kate grinned. "I can't believe I slept so late!"

"Finish your toast."

"It'll be lunchtime soon." She looked at Paul. "How about if we go down to the Country Diner?"

He nodded. "Sure. I'll buy you lunch."

"It's a deal." Kate took a last sip of coffee and ran off to get showered and dressed.

THE COUNTRY DINER was packed. When Kate and Paul walked in, they were hit with a volley of questions.

"Did Junius really try to steal a car?" asked Martha Sinclair.

"Did he really try to make a run for it?" asked Morty Robertson.

"Did someone say something about a gun?" Gail Carson, the local Realtor, asked.

"I heard he had thousands of dollars on him, all stolen from the bank!" Roberta Grant exclaimed.

"He didn't steal a thing from the bank," Georgia Cline snapped. "He stole it from Ada Blount."

"But that was ages ago. He'd have spent all that," Martha objected.

"Jennifer McCarthy wants to do an interview with you," Gail added, holding up her cell phone. "She's on the phone now if you have time."

Kate gasped, then she realized that the barrage of questions weren't aimed at her but at Renee Lambert, who was sitting in state at the counter, Kisses in her arms.

"Maybe later, Gail," Renee said. "But, of course, you know my Kisses was the hero of the day. He chased down that thief in the middle of the casino. You should have seen him, my brave Little Umpkins!"

Kisses sneezed.

LuAnne came up to Paul and Kate. "If you want a table, I think there's a back booth available," she said quietly.

Kate shrunk back. This wasn't what she had in mind. "How long has Renee been here?" she asked.

"All morning. She's in hog heaven." LuAnne made a face. "How much of it's true?"

"Junius is in jail," Kate whispered back. "And she did sic Kisses on him."

LuAnne sniffed. "Well, that's something." Her tone held a hint of hostility.

Some healing needs to take place here, Kate thought.

Paul looked at Kate and said, "LuAnne, I think we're going to go somewhere quieter today."

LuAnne nodded.

"Of course, I never trusted that man for a minute," Renee said loudly as Paul and Kate crept back outside.

"Back home?" Kate asked.

Paul shook his head. "I know a quiet place where you can get a pretty good hamburger. Come on," he said, opening the pickup door for her.

Paul drove to Barnhill Street and turned left. When they crossed the railroad tracks, Kate asked, "Where are we going?"

"The Dew Drop Inn." Paul laughed as Kate raised an eyebrow. "Trust me. It's not bad."

There were only a couple of cars outside the old roadhouse, assuring Kate that it would be a quiet lunch.

She followed Paul inside and heard two men talking.

"Peyton Manning," said one.

"Steve Young," said the other.

When her eyes had adjusted to the dim light, she saw that Matt Lawson was talking with that huge man who ran the place, Bo Twist.

Matt shook his head. "Peyton Manning broke Steve Young's passer rating."

"That's only single season, not career," Bo replied.

"But," Matt said, "Peyton Manning has the most touchdown passes, most career passes—"

"No, consecutive-season passes," Bo interrupted.

"Let the games begin." Paul grinned.

"Hey, Pastor!" Bo called. "Where's the rest of the band?"

"Just me and the wife today," Paul said. "We wanted a quiet lunch."

"Well, you sure weren't the only people with that idea. Matt here said the diner was a regular circus today."

Matt shifted uncomfortably in his chair.

"How are you doing, Matt?" Paul asked.

Matt shrugged. "Okay."

"Why don't you folks sit with Matt and I'll get us all some lunch," Bo said blandly.

"Do you mind?" Kate asked Matt.

"No," Matt said, glancing briefly at Bo. "Please. Sit down."

"What to drink?" Bo asked. "I've got coffee and some sweet tea on tap."

"Tea," Kate said as they sat down.

"Coffee," said Paul.

"Be right back." Bo lumbered off, the floorboards creaking under his feet.

"I didn't know you two knew each other, Matt," Paul said.

"Huh? Who?" Matt asked, looking at Kate, bewildered.

"Bo Twist," Paul added.

"Oh. Yeah. We met at one of the high-school football games last fall. He likes football a lot, like me."

Paul nodded.

"And I also help him with his investments." Matt drank some coffee. "Yeah. He and I . . . we talk every once in a while."

"That's good, Matt. I'm glad to hear it," Paul said.

Kate was amazed at the friendships that could spark between such different people.

"Here you go," Bo said, coming back with their drinks. "Now me and Matt were gonna have hamburgers and fries. Sound good to you two?"

Paul and Kate both nodded.

"I'll just slap a couple more burgers on the grill, then," he said and went off again.

"You didn't have to work today, Matt?" Paul asked, stirring a little packet of sugar into his coffee.

"When I got home last night, I called the bank and left a message on the answering machine that I would be in late today so I could sleep in." He lowered his head. "I didn't want to go straight in and face people."

Bo returned with platters, three of them bearing a hamburger and a huge mound of french fries. The fourth, with two hamburgers on it and an even larger mound of fries, was his.

"Dig in, folks. Oh, and if you'd like to say grace"—Bo looked straight at Paul—"go right ahead. I don't mind."

Paul suppressed a smile and said a blessing, then everyone began eating. The hamburgers were delicious, juicy but not greasy, and the fries were perfect.

"I'm glad you'uns came on out here," Bo said, picking up the last hamburger on his plate. "I know this boy here's been going through a lot, what with watchin' his daddy being arrested and all."

Kate almost gasped at the casual way he said it.

Matt hung his head. "And now it's all over town," he said.

"I know," Bo said, "but you're worryin' way too much." Then he turned to Paul and Kate. "He's got some cocka-mamy idea that this is gonna reflect on him in a bad way. I figure maybe you can talk some sense into him."

Matt looked around, his eyes like a puppy's again. "I like my job. I like Copper Mill. It's quiet. And there aren't too many people. I don't want to have to leave."

"You don't have to go anywhere," Kate exclaimed.

"It's not you that's in trouble," Paul pointed out. "It's your father."

"But people will blame me," Matt said. "They'll think I'm just like him."

Kate took a deep breath and said, "Matt, that's one thing you don't have to worry about. Nobody is going to blame you."

Matt thought for a moment, then asked, "Do you really think I can stay here?"

"Of course you can," Paul assured him. "What your father did isn't your fault."

"That's not what he says," Matt replied.

"What do you mean?" Paul asked.

"Well, the truth is, I'm . . . different," Matt said slowly. "I always have been. I knew that back when I first went to school. I didn't fit in. And I know that people get angry with me and frustrated because I don't do or say what they expect."

"That must be hard," Kate said, biting off the end of a french fry.

Matt was quiet for a moment, then continued, "Mom didn't mind that I'm different. But it drove Dad crazy. It still does. He says that if I wasn't so different, we could hang around together. But we can't and that's why he has to find his fun elsewhere. And sometimes he gets in trouble."

"That's . . . that's nonsense," Kate said, anger surging through her.

"That's just an excuse your father is using to cover up his own behavior," Paul added. "It has nothing to do with you at all. If it wasn't you, he'd find somebody or something else to blame."

"Really?"

"Really," Paul assured him. "People do it all the time. Proverbs 19:3 says, 'A man's own folly ruins his life, yet his heart rages against the Lord.'"

"I knew he'd quote somethin' from the Bible," Bo said casually, finishing the last of his french fries.

"And if they don't blame God, they blame their jobs or their parents or their children," Paul continued. "But those are just excuses. Your father stole and lied and cheated and gambled, and none of it has anything to do with you."

"But Dad—" Matt began, but Bo interrupted him.

"Matt, would you believe what your father says about his finances?"

"No. He always lies about money."

"Then why in tarnation do you believe what he says about you?" Bo asked.

Kate felt like cheering.

Matt was quiet for a moment. "I never thought of it like that," he said.

"Well, if I was you, I'd start thinkin' about it now," Bo said.

"Good advice!" Paul glanced at his watch. "Well, we'd better get going. And any time you want to talk, Matt, just call me."

Matt nodded. "I will. Thank you."

"How much for the burgers?" Paul asked, getting up and reaching for his wallet.

Bo looked up at him and shook his head. "Don't you dare bring out a penny. This one is on the house."

"Thanks," Paul said.

Bo turned toward Matt and said, "Now, I still say that career passes trumps consecutive . . ."

JOE ANSWERED THE DOOR at Amanda's house and Kate smiled with delight to see him there.

"Kate! Come on in," he said, gesturing for her to enter.

"Kate!" Amanda cried.

She started to rise, but Kate protested, "Don't you dare get up. I just wanted to see how you're doing."

"Just fine, now that she knows we didn't rob her blind," Joe said.

"Sit down, Kate," Amanda said. "Joe, would you mind putting the kettle on and making us all some tea? We never did have our tea last night."

"No, we didn't," Kate said. "I'm sorry."

"I'm not," Amanda replied. "I'm glad you found out the truth about Junius and that you got him. The nerve of that man! And that reminds me," she added. "I was told all about the scarf and it's sitting on my bureau. Please take it back. If I had only known . . . Why didn't you tell me?"

"Well, to be honest, you had just had a heart attack," Kate said.

Amanda chuckled. "I suppose that isn't the ideal time to tell someone that her suitor's a crook." She patted Kate's hand. "I understand."

"Here's tea!" Joe said, bringing in a tray loaded with teapot, cups, creamer, and sugar bowl. "Needs to steep a minute, but we can wait."

"Well, good," Amanda said. "Sit yourself down, Joe, and don't loom over people."

Kate stifled a smile, looking at Joe's slight figure.

"So, Junius took Ada Blount's money," Amanda said

calmly. "I heard this morning that Mabel Trout's silver creamer was found in a box marked quilt scraps and no one has any idea how it got there, least of all Mabel."

Kate nodded. "Mindy's necklace was found in Junius' apartment. And this morning Renee told Betty that her ring has been turned in as evidence. As far as Ada's rhinestone brooch, well, I have a feeling that's going to be turned in as evidence as well."

"Oh good," Amanda said, smiling.

"If you don't mind my asking, did Junius ever ask you for any investment funds?"

"No," Amanda replied, "but I'm sure he was working up to it. Although he'd have had a sore disappointment in me. I've had experience with bad eggs."

There was a sudden, heavy silence.

"I've changed," Joe said softly.

"Yes, I know you have," Amanda said apologetically. "I was talking about my brother, Bob." She sighed deeply. "Truth is, compared to him, you were an angel. Yes, you cleaned his pockets of money that wasn't his. But Bob was the one sitting there with a wallet full of payroll money. Did you ever wonder what he was doing with it?"

"No," Joe said. "I never thought about it."

"I did," Amanda said. "And I asked him about it. You should have seen his face! And the spluttering he did . . . That's when I knew what he really was. He'd taken that money specifically to gamble with, and if you hadn't shown up, he'd have gambled it with somebody else. No, you might have tempted him, but he fell all on his own."

Amanda looked down at her hands. "It took me a long time to realize that. I blamed everybody in the world for Bob's faults, when he was the one who committed them. But then, he was my childhood hero."

"I'm sorry," Joe said.

Amanda nodded and turned to Kate. "Kate, would you mind getting the graham crackers out of the kitchen cabinet?"

"Of course," Kate said, fetching them and putting some on a small plate.

"I always like a graham cracker with my afternoon tea," Amanda said when Kate returned with the plate. She picked up a cracker, snapped it in quarters, and dipped one quarter in her tea.

She glanced at Joe every once in a while in a way that made Kate apprehensive.

"The money you sent," Amanda said suddenly. "To repay Bob? He pocketed it. He'd already repaid the bank with the money out of my college fund."

"No!" Joe cried. "And you never got to college?"

"I did indeed go to college," Amanda said, wiping her fingers on her napkin. "I didn't graduate, but that's because I got married. The only difference is, I worked my way through instead of having it all paid for. But I think it was good for me. I got to know what it was like to live on a paycheck." She smiled ruefully. "That's something I didn't know back when you and I were seeing each other."

"But Bob took your money and never paid you back?" Joe asked.

Amanda nodded. "He told the bank he'd lost the wallet somewhere. And then, once he'd gotten my college money—"

"How did he do that?" Joe interrupted.

"We-ell," Amanda said reluctantly. "Bob was executor of Daddy's will, not to mention chief beneficiary, so he could actually do anything he wanted with the money. But that money was earmarked for me and he did do me the honor of asking me to help him out first. And I agreed. Partly because I was so angry with you."

Joe winced.

"So he got the money and went trotting back to the bank and told them he'd found the wallet. I'm still surprised they believed him, but I think we were more naive in those days, don't you? I certainly was. Or perhaps the bank just didn't want the scandal. I certainly didn't want that either."

"But why didn't he pay you back?" Joe persisted.

"Because he didn't have to," Amanda said. "I'm his sister. Besides, I didn't even know about the money you'd sent him until long after Walter and I were married. Mama told me when I came home to take care of her when she was dying."

Amanda was silent for a moment, then she sighed. "I kept waiting for him to come back, but he never did. And to be taken in by Junius after all that . . ."

"Amanda, it's perfectly understandable," Joe said.

"I was flattered and I enjoyed it," Amanda replied. "He flirted with me, gave me compliments and presents.

Stolen ones, but presents. The truth is, it was my pride that was involved, not my heart. It may be silly, but being a woman stays with you well into old age. And sometimes you want to feel attractive, even when you're wrinkled and gray and arthritic."

"Don't say that," Joe said. "You're the most beautiful woman I've ever known. You always have been and you always will be."

"Joe!" Amanda protested.

"It's true. You're the only woman I've ever loved. Don't you know that? I love you. I'll always love you."

They reached out for each other, touched, and held hands. Kate could almost see time peeling away from them. Quietly she got up, picked up her purse, and went to the door. She paused at the door and looked back at them. They were sitting together, hands entwined, looking deeply into each other's eyes.

Thank God that old wounds can be healed by love. She softly closed the door behind her and headed home.

Chapter Eighteen

I t was a warm summer evening when Kate found herself walking across the Town Green. The sun was just beginning to sink below the tops of the trees, and the air was still, dry, and sweet. Birds chirped in the trees and squirrels raced each other along the branches. People were already filling the park benches that had been arranged in a semicircle around the small platform stage. The town clock tolled 6:45. The first installment of the Copper Mill summer concert series would begin at seven.

"Kate!" Livvy called out. "Over here!"

Kate waved and walked to where her friend was seated. "What a beautiful evening," she said.

"Isn't it? I think we're going to get quite a turnout. Where's Paul?"

"Oh, he's here somewhere," Kate said, looking around. She didn't want to say any more lest she give away the surprise the quartet had been working so hard on.

On the other side of Livvy sat Martha Sinclair, Dot Bagley, and Renee's mother, Caroline Beauregard Johnston.

All three women spooned ice cream from plastic cups as they talked. Kate craned her neck, and sure enough, there was the Elk's fund-raiser stand by the trees, with Mayor Briddle, Joe Tucker, and Eli Weston dishing up ice cream beneath a big banner that read "Root-Beer Floats! Two dollars each!"

"I see Joe raised the price of the floats," Kate commented.

"The mayor did that," Livvy said. "He said a dollar wasn't enough to pay for the ice cream, much less make a profit."

Kate nodded. "Shall we get one?"

"Oh yes, let's," Livvy said. "We've got time."

They got up and walked through the rows of benches, exchanging greetings with folks as they went.

"Y'all aren't taking off yet, are you?" Skip Spencer asked as they came to the end of a row.

"No, Skip," Kate assured him. "We're just going to get a root-beer float."

"Good. 'Cause we've got something really special lined up for tonight!" Skip grinned and went on down the row, where he homed in on a young woman with long red hair.

Kate got in line behind Lester Philpott and looked down the line. Marissa Harris was standing with Jack Wilson, both of them with eyes only for each other. Kate saw Joe take a root-beer float over to a nearby bench where Amanda was sitting. He handed it to her with a courtly bow, shaking his head when she began to fumble in her purse. Then he zipped back to the booth and continued his work. Amanda took a bite of ice cream, smiling happily.

"How is it?" Kate called to Amanda.

"Scrumptious!" Amanda replied.

"Overpriced!" Old Man Parsons added from behind Livvy.

"You should know," Amanda responded tartly. "You've had two and now you're in line for a third."

Old Man Parsons grunted. "Well," he said to Kate and Livvy, "it's for charity, isn't it?"

"That's right," Kate said, stepping up to the booth.

"Two root-beer floats for the ladies!" Joe called back to Eli.

"How are sales going?" Kate asked.

"Couldn't be better," Joe replied. "We're going to raise a decent pile of money with these."

Eli handed the floats to Joe, who passed them to Kate and Livvy. "Here you go, ladies. Hope you enjoy them!"

"Kate, can I talk to you for a moment?" Amanda asked as Kate was passing by, touching Kate's arm lightly.

Kate gestured to Livvy to go on without her, then walked with Amanda toward a grove of trees. Kate suspected that whatever Amanda wanted to say, she wanted to do it privately.

"I wanted to let you know I'm leaving," Amanda said, pursing her lips.

"Leaving?" Kate repeated, dazed. She felt a little silly, but she couldn't quite make sense of what Amanda had just said.

"I'm moving back to Knoxville to be closer to my children," Amanda continued quickly. "After the heart attack," she said, reaching up to pat her perfectly styled hair, "I realized I can't take anything for granted. I miss my family. I want to see my grandchildren grow up."

"B-but . . ." Kate stammered. How could Amanda leave now? "But what about . . ."

"Joe?" Amanda asked, blushing. "I'll still see Joe as much as possible. Who knows what might happen? I do know that God has worked mightily in bringing us back together after so many years and I can't believe he's going to stop working now."

"I suppose that's true." Kate bit her lip, trying to figure out what to say. "But Amanda . . ." she sighed. "We're going to miss you!"

"You're sweet." Amanda patted Kate's arm. "But I know this is the right thing. And don't you worry; I'll be back to visit all the time."

Amanda looked over to where Joe was serving root-beer floats and smiled. "Anyway, I just wanted to thank you for all you've done for me. Without you, all of this would have turned out differently."

"I'm just glad I could help." Kate took a sip of her float and smiled as the fizzy liquid trickled down her throat.

"It looks like the show is about to start," Amanda said, gesturing toward the stage, where Lester Philpott was testing the microphones.

"Shall we?" Kate asked, holding out her arm to Amanda.

"You go on ahead." Amanda smiled. "I'm going to sit with Joe."

"Oh fine," Kate said, laughing. "Now you be good," she teased as she walked away.

She rejoined Livvy and was surprised to run into Matt Lawson. Behind him was Bo Twist.

"Hello, Mrs. Hanlon," Bo said.

"Hello, Bo. How are you doing?" Kate asked.

"Pretty well," he said, poking Matt in the arm.

Matt looked at him, startled, and then said, "Hello, Kate, Livvy. How are you doing tonight?"

"Just fine," Kate said.

"Great, Matt," Livvy replied. "How are you?"

"I'm doing fine." Matt glanced at Bo, who smiled.

"Come on, Son," Bo said, "let's get us a couple of floats and go find a place to sit down."

Kate watched them go. They were an odd duo, but their relationship definitely seemed to be blossoming into a true friendship. She could see that Bo was helping Matt navigate the difficult world of social interaction.

"God works in mysterious ways," Kate said aloud as Joe darted past them, heading toward the Mercantile.

"Oh, here comes Danny," Livvy said. "Let's take our seats."

"When is James's band on?" Kate asked her.

"The garage bands are always on last," Livvy assured her. "That's so the older folks can go home and protect their ears."

Danny Jenner got up on the small stage, microphone

in hand. "Ladies and gentlemen. Welcome to the first evening of the Copper Mill summer concert series! We've got a tremendous lineup of music and performers for you here tonight, but I want everyone out there to remember, there's always room for more. I want to see more participants next week. And I want to see you keep drinking those root-beer floats!"

Everyone laughed.

"Remember, all the money's going to a good cause. So, sit back and enjoy yourselves. And now, our concert opener. A brand new group, the Copper Mill Kazoo Players!"

The quacking sound of kazoos came from behind them. Kate turned and gasped as Paul, Sam, Skip, and Joe came winding their way through the crowd, all of them wearing straw boater hats and red-striped shirts, as if they were in a barbershop quartet. She was laughing with delight even before they made it to the stage, still playing "Stars and Stripes Forever."

Everyone in the audience rose to their feet, cheering, laughing, and applauding when the quartet bowed. Paul was grinning from ear to ear. They played two more marching-band numbers and took a final bow before their wildly enthusiastic audience.

Danny came back up on stage, laughing. "And they've promised, folks, to be a part of the homecoming parade this fall!"

Everyone cheered.

"And now let's give a big welcome to the Pine Ridge Jazz Ensemble!"

As the band assembled onstage, Paul came and sat down beside Kate, who was still breathless from laughing.

"So, how'd you like it?" he asked. He was still grinning from ear to ear.

"You . . . It was wonderful!" Kate beamed at him.

"You guys were great," Livvy said, laughing.

"Thanks."

Paul sat back with relief and happiness as the community band played. The setting sun threw longer and longer shadows onto the grass. At one point Kate glanced behind her and saw Joe sitting beside Amanda.

The community band finished and Skip Spencer came up next, banjo in hand. He put it over his shoulder, shook a lock of red hair back from his forehead, and began playing a fast, furious version of "Foggy Mountain Breakdown." When he was done, everybody roared and clapped. Then he began singing "Wildwood Flower."

Livvy leaned over and said quietly in Kate's ear, "That boy can sing."

Kate nodded. Skip's tenor voice was beautiful. When he finished and everyone applauded, Kate saw a red-haired girl standing, clapping wildly. Skip had scored a hit.

"Who knew he could sing?" Danny asked as Skip left the stage. "Now, folks, it's my pleasure to announce what I think, no, I know, is everyone's favorite group. Copper Mill's one and only Beauty Shop Quartet!"

Everyone cheered as Renee, LuAnne, Betty, and Emma stepped up onstage. Tears came to Kate's eyes as she saw Renee take LuAnne's hand as the four began singing "Keep on the Sunny Side."

"It's good to see them back together," Livvy said.

"Amen," Kate replied. It was all she could say.

The women's voices harmonized beautifully. After two more old country favorites, Betty took the microphone and said, "Thank you, all of you. We appreciate it so much. Now we're going to do one final number. And anyone who feels like joining in, please do, as we sing 'I'll Fly Away.'"

Kate was too happy to sing. She sat there smiling, breathing in the soft night air as the sun set, the fireflies darted around the Town Green and the voices of her friends and neighbors rose into the night.

About the Author

EVE FISHER began writing while in elementary school, and her mystery stories have appeared regularly in *Alfred Hitchcock Mystery Magazine* for the last ten years. Although she currently lives in a small town in South Dakota, in a house that she shares with her husband, cat and five thousand books, she spent seven years in the mountains of Tennessee in a town remarkably like Copper Mill. She hopes the readers will feel at home in Copper Mill as she has. Besides writing mysteries, Eve teaches history at a local university, reads voraciously and bakes constantly.

Mystery and the Minister's Wife

Through the Fire
by Diane Noble

A State of Grace
by Traci DePree

A Test of Faith
by Carol Cox

The Best Is Yet to Be
by Eve Fisher